# RUTHLESS SAINTS

## BOOK ONE SOLD TO THE MAFIA BOSS

### ELLA JADE

*Ruthless Saints* © 2022 Ella Jade

Editor: Zero Alchemy

Cover Designer: Dark City Designs

Photographer: Eric Battershell

Cover Model: Johnny Kane

All rights reserved under the International and Pan-American Copyright Conventions. No part of this book may be reproduced or transmitted in any form or by any means, electronic or mechanical, including photocopying, recording, or by any information storage and retrieval system, without permission in writing from the publisher.

This is a work of fiction. Names, places, characters and incidents are either the product of the author's imagination or are used fictitiously, and any resemblance to any actual persons, living or dead, organizations, events or locales is entirely coincidental.

Warning: the unauthorized reproduction or distribution of this copyrighted work is illegal. Criminal copyright infringement, including infringement without monetary gain, is investigated by the FBI and is punishable by up to 5 years in prison and a fine of $250,000.

http://authorellajade.com/

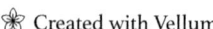 Created with Vellum

# NOTE FROM THE AUTHOR

*"The only difference between the saint and the sinner is that every saint has a past, and every sinner has a future."* Oscar Wilde

Thank you for checking out this series. It's dark, edgy, and pushes some limits.

**CHAPTER 1**

*Luciana*

When you're in the moment, things can seem bleak. Be careful what you wish for because the future might not be the brighter option.

"Hold that fucking door!" a man yelled from across the busy Manhattan street.

Startled, I jostled where I stood, scalding tea spilling out the top of my cup and trickling down my wrist. "Ouch!"

*Damn it. That burned!*

"Lu!" My cousin Vincent, who had been the one yelling for me to hold the front door of the firm's offices, came up from behind me. "Now."

I glanced over my shoulder to find him and his brother Rocco dragging a badly beaten man in from the sidewalk. Bright red blood poured out of his nose and splattered onto his white dress shirt. His swollen left eye held a purple hue and he could hardly open it, but he tried to stare at me through the injury.

I pressed my back against the door, holding it and trying

to stay out of their way as they lugged the unfortunate man into the law firm.

They hurried toward the back offices toward the rooms we didn't use for everyday business.

My cousin Alessandro winked at me as he followed his brothers down the hall.

"Sandro, you can sit this one out," Rocco snapped before he dashed into the office.

He slammed the door shut, and I jumped, spilling more tea down my hand.

Alessandro, the youngest of the trio, followed me into my tiny workspace. It was actually the firm's law library, but I'd set up a makeshift office when my Uncle Antonio brought me on as a paralegal last summer. It wasn't the most prestigious spot in the building, but it suited me fine.

The area smelled of old books, and I loved reading all the case studies. I wanted to go to law school like my cousins had, but my uncle wouldn't allow it. The best I could do was get him to agree to let me become a paralegal, so I attended the local community college.

I wasn't giving up on my dreams yet. I could still go to law school if I could find a way out of here. This wasn't the kind of family a person could walk away from. I'd have to get creative if I wanted out.

I set what was left of my tea on my desk and grabbed a tissue from the box on the window sill to wipe my hand and wrist.

Sandro sat on the edge of my desk, straightening his new Armani tie. "Typical Monday morning, huh?"

"So it seems." I powered up my computer. "Only in New York City could three attorneys drag a half-dead man into a law firm and no one bats an eyelash."

"Not if those attorneys' last name is Torrio they don't."

*Torrio* was synonymous with the most powerful mafia family on the East coast. My uncle and his sons ran the New York organization right out of their legitimate law firm. They had prestigious and influential clients coming in and out of this place all day long, and no one questioned their motives or dangerous dealings, including me. I kept my head down like an obedient dog. That was how I had survived since coming to live with this menacing family when my parents died.

"Want to go to lunch at that cafe you like today?" Sandro asked. "They have chicken salad on the menu again."

"I have to draft those court documents your dad needs, and I have all that filing to do." I motioned toward the stack of folders on the corner of my desk. "Don't you have to work?"

"We can take a lunch break," he reminded me. "You know what they say about all work and no play."

"You play enough." I logged onto my computer. "You didn't make it home last night. I waited for you."

"I went to the club and met up with someone I knew from high school. She kept me quite busy." He smirked. "All night and this morning too."

"You could have texted me." I shrugged, trying not to show my hurt. Sandro was two years older than me. When I came to live with them, he became a good friend to me. Vincent and Rocco were older and took on the roles of protective brothers, but Sandro and I had a special bond. "I worried about you."

"You don't have to worry about me, Lu." He laughed. "No one is going to fuck with me."

"Because you're a Torrio?"

"Exactly. And so are you."

"I don't always feel like one."

Maybe it was their way of life I couldn't understand. They shielded me from most of it, even sending me away to a prestigious boarding school in Connecticut during high school, but I knew there were sinister things happening under the roof they provided for me. Some things couldn't be unseen. Like the man they had in the back offices. What were they doing to him? Had they beaten him or had a rival family? No matter how much I wanted to live a normal life under ordinary circumstances, being a Torrio, even if it wasn't my birth name, had cursed me to a world of danger and violence.

"You are one of us, Lu," Sandro said. "I know my mom doesn't always treat you like you are, but my brothers and I do our best to include you."

"I know." Aunt Kristina wasn't the most maternal woman I'd ever met. She was so different from my mom. My mother was kind and gentle and loved me with all her heart. When I came to live here, I tried to get close to my aunt, but she never let me in. After a few years, I stopped trying. Our relationship was icy. "I love all of you, but I think it's time for a change, you know?"

"What kind of change?" He slipped off my desk and gazed out the window. "You know how things are around here. We have routines. We can't afford surprises."

"I've been thinking more about law school. I have my associate's degree and I've been working here for almost a year. I might ask your dad if I could finish my degree."

"He might allow that."

"I want to check out schools away from here."

"Now *that* he'll never let it happen." He turned to face me. "You know that."

"Why?"

"He wants us all close to home, especially now." He grabbed the back of the chair and squeezed, "Trust me. Don't ask him to send you to law school away from here. It won't go well."

"What do you mean, *especially now*?"

"There are things happening behind the scenes... Sorry, that's all I can say."

"With the family business?"

"I've already said too much."

"I'll take that as a yes, then, and be glad you can't say more. I don't want to know about that stuff. I want to branch out and see who I can be *away* from here."

"Why would you want to get away? You have a good life —a nice-paying job, a wealthy, powerful family to protect you."

"Why do I need protection?" I crossed my arms. The fact that I would need protection should make it pretty clear why I'd want to get out of here. "I have nothing to do with the 'family business.' I work in a legitimate law firm. I want to be a lawyer like you, Vincent, and Rocco. Why can't I pursue that? I'm twenty-two years old and, except for that sheltered boarding school, I haven't gone anywhere or seen anything. Your parents keep me locked in the castle. I don't even have friends."

"What am I?"

"You know what I mean." I walked around my desk and joined him at the window. "There's an entire world out there, and I want to see it. I want to live."

"I know it's difficult living with us."

"That's an understatement." I rolled my eyes. "Don't you understand why I want to get away? You and your brothers have always been a part of this world. I don't belong here. I never did, Alessandro. I don't understand any of it, and I don't want to."

"You do belong here." He turned to face me. "Where is all of this coming from?"

"I don't know. I guess I've been feeling restless. You're going out so much these days and I'm at home. I'm lonely and I don't know what my purpose is."

"Your purpose is here with us, Lu. It always has been." He patted my back. "You'll find your place in this family. Keep working hard here. My father will see how worthy you are. He'll let you get your law degree, but right now, he has a lot on his plate. I promise, I'll help you convince him to let you go back to school when the time is right."

"Thank you." I smiled. "You've always been my best friend."

"You're mine too." He kissed my cheek. "I'll swing back here in an hour and we'll go to lunch. I won't take no for an answer."

"I wouldn't expect anything less from you." I pointed to the hallway. "Go, so I can do my work."

"You'll have lunch with me?"

"Yes."

"Sandro!" Rocco yelled from his office down the hall. "Get in here."

"I better go," he said. "I don't want to make the beast mad."

"Like I didn't fucking hear that?" Rocco shouted. "Lu, send me the Canter file."

"Okay." I had already sent it to him twice yesterday, but I wouldn't dare tell him that. It was easier to resend it. "I'm doing it now."

"Thank you." He practically grunted the words before slamming his door.

Rocco was an intimidating man, but he could be gentle when the situation called for it. Vincent, on the other hand, was scarier and rarely said thank you. He barked orders and could make me cry if I didn't do exactly what he asked. I tried my best to make sure I never screwed things up for him.

I sat at my desk, pulling up the file Rocco needed and emailing it to him. I glanced at the stack of folders, but I wasn't in the mood to put them away. My conversation with Sandro had left me discouraged.

I had been planning on talking to my uncle about law school for weeks, but I couldn't get up the nerve to ask him. Sandro didn't give me any extra confidence, but maybe it was time for me to start thinking on my own and looking at the bigger picture.

In a regular family, a twenty-two-year-old woman could leave home if she wanted. I'd been saving money from this job since I'd started. They paid me a salary for tax purposes, but I didn't need the paycheck. My uncle provided me with a daily allowance. He had for years.

But even with my paychecks being deposited into my account, I didn't have any real independence. I lived under his roof. He paid for my car, phone, clothes, and food. I rarely went out, and when I did, it was usually with Sandro or Rocco, and they paid for everything.

There were many nights I thought about leaving. It would feel more like an escape because I'd have to get past the house security and the guard who was assigned to tail me. My uncle said Sam was for my protection, but he made me feel more like a prisoner. I had lived this way for so long, I wasn't sure I could adjust out in the world by myself.

Still, I wanted to at least *try*.

I wanted to meet people my age. Go on trips. Have drinks with girlfriends.

Dates would be nice too. I hadn't been on many of those. Most guys ran in the opposite direction when they found out my last name.

I wanted to be a normal girl with a normal family and a normal life. Was that really too much to ask? I couldn't help being part of this family because I was born into it. I wouldn't hurt them or betray them. Despite the odd relationship, I loved them. But I wanted to be treated like an adult who had hopes and dreams. Not like a lowly niece who they took in because they had no choice.

It was time for me to take a stand and tell them what I wanted. I had obeyed and did what they told me to do. I'd been a good little girl, but now it was time to be a woman—no matter what the consequences might be.

Standing from my chair, I took a deep breath and convinced myself I could do this. I could find my voice and demand my freedom.

As I headed for the door, my uncle appeared in front of me, tall, overbearing, and terrifying. When he spoke, people stopped what they were doing and listened. I was no exception.

He leaned against one of the large mahogany bookcases. "Where are you going?"

"I... um... I was on my way to see you." I backed away from him. "I mean, if you're not too busy."

"Perfect timing." He placed his large hand on the small of my back. "Come with me."

He guided me down the hall.

"Is everything okay?"

"We need to have a conversation."

"Oh." I swallowed hard as my three cousins stood

outside of Rocco's office, staring as their father led me to his office. My stomach churned and my legs trembled as I slowly put one foot in front of the other. I couldn't think of one positive reason why he would want to speak with me.

*Why do I feel like I'm heading to the electric chair?*

**CHAPTER 2**

*Romero*

Gazing out of my penthouse windows, I realized I had New York City at my fingertips. The power flowed through my veins. It had taken me years to get to this point, but I did it.

When I was eighteen years old, someone brutally murdered my father while he sat in his car in front of our family home. He'd created an empire and it all could have been mine, but I'd walked away because I didn't know who I could trust. I was young and wasn't ready to run such an established business. My father's shoes were too big to fill. If they could murder the head of a notorious crime family in front of his house, any of us were fair game. So, I went underground and bided my time, creating my own dynasty.

If I was being totally honest, filling my father's shoes wasn't something I particularly wanted. I didn't want to be like him. He was a vicious bastard who didn't know how to be a husband or a father. I'd spent years trying to please him, but I never could. When he died, it set me free. Some of the other families looked down on me because I didn't fight for his territory or try to avenge his death. Those two things weren't important to me. What I had today was much more valuable. My business was something no one could take away from me.

Fifteen years later, I was back, having clawed my way to the top with the help of my younger brother, Gio. Together, there wasn't anything we couldn't accomplish. Our allies respected us, and our enemies feared us. It poised us to finally stand in our father's place, but now it would be on our own merits. The Bilotti last name was a useful asset, but now when we walked into a room, people saw us as a force to be reckoned with.

Nothing could stop us from gaining control of the organization that was rightfully ours. Alliances needed to be made to strengthen our position if we wanted to peacefully move products through the harbors. Once everything fell into place, there would be no stopping us.

"Romero." Gio stepped out of the elevator and joined me by the window. He said nothing as he looked down at the bustling city below us. If he was quiet, it meant we had a problem.

"What brings you here so early in the afternoon?"

"We might have an issue."

"Those aren't the words I want to hear coming from your mouth." I relied on him to make sure all the problems were taken care of before they reached my desk.

"Believe me, I could think of a hundred other things I'd rather tell you."

Gio ran the day-to-day operations of the business because he had more patience with people. I handled negotiations and made others see things my way. He was extremely efficient at his job and seldom came to me with problems.

I didn't like where this was headed.

"What is it?" I asked.

"Arturo isn't answering his texts," Gio said. "I'm concerned."

Arturo was one of our high-ranking lieutenants. One I would trust with my life. We'd given him some of the most important and dangerous jobs to carry out, and he always did with the utmost precision.

"Where was he last?" I walked around the sofa, still gazing out at the bustling city below me.

"He was on assignment in New Jersey, overseeing that shipment."

"The one we agreed he was the only one we would trust with such a sensitive cargo and now we can't find him?"

"I haven't heard from him since last night." Gio checked his phone. "It seems off."

"Could he have gone underground for security reasons?"

My men were resourceful. I'd taught them how to stay out of sight and protect what was mine. If Arturo felt a rival family was on his trail or worse yet, the Feds had picked up his movements, he would know to lie low.

"It's possible, but he rarely goes totally off the grid."

"It hasn't been twenty-four hours yet." Things didn't always go according to plan. Arturo had excellent instincts. If he sensed a problem, I had total faith he would back off until they could move my shipment without an issue. "I wouldn't panic."

"When do you ever panic?"

"If I did, it could get us killed. A man doesn't get this far in life, especially in this business, without balls of steel. Do we have any information?"

"This might not be related, but our source says Antonio

Torrio has been sniffing around and asking questions about us. Do you think he could have something to do with this?"

"I sure as fuck hope not because then I'll have to retaliate and that isn't something I'm looking to do at this time." I clenched my fist because Torrio was no small-time thug. A feud with him would end in massive bloodshed. "There are too many balls in the air. We have too much going on. I don't need to make any enemies, especially not in the city."

Torrio had been running things since our father's death. I had hoped he would be a useful ally. He had contacts and connections in the city that would be beneficial to me. He also had three capable sons who knew how to handle all sorts of shit. Having a family like that on my side could only strengthen my presence.

"I know you're hoping we can work with him, but I'm not sure we can trust him." Gio went into the kitchen and returned a few moments later with two bottles of water. "Have you changed your mind?"

"I never said I would trust him, but if I can create an alliance with him, we could expand our territory."

"How much more do we need?" He tossed me a water bottle.

"Thank you," I said as I caught the bottle. "We didn't come this far to stop now."

Torrio had gotten in my way a few times over the past few years. He was particular about his territory and didn't always allow unestablished entities to run their merchandise through his ports. His men let me go a couple times because of my last name. They claimed it was out of respect for my father, but Antonio made it clear he didn't have that same tolerance for me. The smug bastard and his ice queen wife had an air about them. Like their shit didn't stink. They wanted me to earn their respect, but I didn't earn anything I didn't deem necessary. If I wanted something, I took it. Torrio and his clan were no different. I wouldn't let them stand in my way. We would either work together or I would eliminate them.

"I wonder what you'll have to do to make that alliance." Gio stepped away from the window, fidgeting with his watch. "You don't need to compromise yourself."

"Don't worry, little brother. I never do anything I don't want to, and I'll never negotiate anything if I don't come out better on the other side. I'll only ever do what benefits us."

"You've gotten us this far."

"I intend to get us all the way to the top."

That wasn't a dream. It was a promise. Years ago, some of the most revered mobsters had laughed at me for even trying to accomplish what I had set out to do. Today, they weren't laughing. Most of them were trying to learn from me. Others were keeping their heads down, hoping I didn't come for their territory.

I was an honorable man. My motto was *don't fuck with me and I won't fuck with you. But not even God himself can help you if you betray me.*

"What do you want me to do about Arturo?" Gio checked his phone. "Should I give it a few more hours?"

"See what you can find out." I headed down the hall to my study. "If Antonio had something to do with this, we'll make him pay."

"It would be a stupid move on his part and he doesn't strike me as a stupid man."

"We all make mistakes and have lapses in judgment. He may have underestimated us and if that's the case, he's going to answer with his life."

"Don't go killing off the head don before I get back with

proof." Gio laughed. "Your temper has a tendency to get the better of you."

"That's why I let you handle the people." I waved to him when he stepped into the elevator. "I can't deal with all that stupidity."

"I'll touch base with you in a few hours."

"Stay safe," I said as the elevator doors closed.

As I stepped into my study, my phone rang inside my pocket. Most people texted me these days, but there were a few exceptions. When I pulled out my cell, the screen displayed the name of my father's former second in command. Giancarlo Vannetti had been like an uncle to me and Gio. He didn't hide his disappointment when I walked away, but he had supported every choice I made since then. He had been a tremendous asset to me and helped counsel me on many deals.

"Giancarlo," I answered. "How are you?"

"I'm well," he replied. "I'm happy you answered."

"I'll always answer for you."

"I'm glad to hear that." He snickered. "You may also be glad when you hear what I have to say."

"Well, if you think I'm going to be glad it must be something good." I needed some positive information after Gio's visit.

"Very good."

"Don't keep me waiting." I took a seat behind my desk, eager to hear what he had to say. "What do you have for me?"

"I've found a way for you to expand your territory and get everything your father had and more."

"I'm listening."

"A deal is being negotiated and you're in a perfect position to accept the terms."

I was confident Giancarlo wouldn't waste my time by coming to me with a shit deal. If he thought it was the right move, I would go with his instincts.

"You'll benefit in many ways," he said.

"What do I have to do?"

"Get married."

## CHAPTER 3

*Luciana*

As I walked to Uncle Antonio's office, suddenly my big, brave moment didn't seem like such a good idea. Sandro was right. Now wasn't the time to tell him I wanted to leave the family and go to law school.

When we entered his office, my aunt was already there, sitting behind his desk. My stomach dropped. Even though we lived in the same house, I tried to avoid her as much as possible. We ate meals together, but we didn't hold meaningful conversations. There was a time when she would talk about my mother and didn't present her in the best light. My uncle quickly put a stop to it, but I got the impression Kristina and my mom were not friends. Perhaps my aunt resented me for being my mother's daughter. Maybe it irritated her that I was the spitting image of my mom. I'd given up trying to figure it out. We would never get along and I was fine with that.

"Come in, *bella*," my uncle said. "We have some things to discuss."

*Bella?* It wasn't often he called me beautiful.

"Hello, Lu," my aunt said, but didn't bother to look at me. "Are you having a good day?"

*Not really.* "Yes."

"Sit down." My uncle motioned to the leather couch across from his desk.

I did as he said. Before he took a seat on the same sofa, he poured himself a glass of water from the pitcher on the table in the corner of the room and took his time to drink it. My nerves intensified as I waited to hear what they wanted. I felt like they had summoned me to the principal's office and I had no idea what I had done. I'd never actually been in trouble before. Even in boarding school, I kept to myself and minded my business. But if someone had called me to the main office, I imagined this was what it would be like.

"You're not in trouble, Lu." My uncle patted my knee. "I've called you here for something positive."

"Oh." Relief washed over me.

"I need your help with something, and I believe you're the only one who can accomplish this very important mission."

*Mission?*

"Our family needs you. I know you won't fail us."

"Your uncle is placing a lot of faith in you." My aunt tapped her long, red fingernails on the oak of the desk. "I'm not sure you're completely up for the task."

"Nonsense." My uncle raised his voice. "I'll have no more talk like that, Kristina."

"Fine." She shook her head, annoyed by my presence, but what else was new? "Tell her what you want."

"I've decided you should start earning your keep in this family." His dark eyes held me captive. "I've kept you sheltered because that was what was best, but now I have the perfect job for you."

"I thought I was earning my keep." I kept my voice soft and steady, but I was on the verge of tears because I seemed to have let him down. I always did what he asked me to do and tried not to be a burden. "I try my best here at the firm."

"You do a fantastic job, but that's not what I mean when I say earning your keep." He sighed. "I know you're not that naïve, Lu. You know who we are and what we're capable of. You read the papers and search the internet. We're not just lawyers here, and you're savvy enough to know that."

"And if she's not," Aunt Kristina chimed in, "then she's definitely not up for this task."

With one stern look from her husband, she backed down. The more my aunt said I wasn't up for this mysterious job, the more I wanted to accept it. How bad could it be? I'd put up with her for years.

"What do you need me to do?" I wanted to get this over with so I could go back to my filing.

"That's my girl." He smiled. "We have a unique opportunity that will advance this family's presence and make all the other families know we're in charge and we're here to stay."

"Has there been a threat?"

My uncle was right. I wasn't completely unaware of how things worked around here. I may not have been included in conversations, but I heard my uncle and cousins talking. Others tried to take over or steal territory all the time.

"Not at all, but sometimes I have to act before a threat even occurs. I've been presented with an alliance that will benefit us and that's where you come in."

I couldn't imagine what I could do to help a mafia alliance, but he had never asked me for help before. Maybe if I agreed to whatever this was, I'd be in a better position to ask about law school. If I helped him, he would owe me. *Right?*

"Are you familiar with Romero Bilotti?"

"I know who he is." Everyone knew who he was: a ruthless arms dealer with a reputation that gave people nightmares. "I saw him at that wedding we went to last month."

"Yes, he was there and the center of attention, if I remember correctly," my aunt said. "You caught his eye at the bar."

How did she know that?

I tried to ignore her comment, but she wasn't wrong. I had gone to the bar to get a drink. Romero sat at the corner talking to another man when I ordered. As soon as I spoke, he switched his attention to me. I gazed in his direction because the weight of his stare called to me. It was bold, and he made no attempt to hide the fact that he was checking me out. He had the most stunning green eyes. I looked away, embarrassed that I had given into his gawking. No one had ever looked at me that way before. It unsettled me. Even after a month, I still thought about that brief exchange that meant nothing to him but filled my lonely nights with something other than books and binge watching shows I'd already seen.

"I saw the way he looked at you," my aunt continued. "I didn't forget that when we negotiated this alliance."

"What do I have to do with this alliance?" I turned to my uncle. "How can I help with Romero?"

"I don't trust him," he said.

"Then why are you making an alliance with him? Don't you have to trust him for something like that?" That made good business sense. Why get involved with someone who could stab you in the back—literally.

"It can become a strong and useful union in the future,

but first I have to be absolutely sure he won't betray me. The joining of the Torrio and Bilotti families can benefit us all, but I have to be careful. I have to know this isn't a trap."

I shifted in my seat, eager to hear how I figured into any of this.

"I need you to bring me information."

"On Bilotti? You want me to research him?" I let out a deep breath because this assignment didn't sound that awful. "I'm good at that."

"I know you are," my uncle said. "It will be a little more involved than researching him. As I said, this is a job I can only let you handle. I'm putting a lot of faith in you, but I know you won't fail me."

My aunt bit her lip so hard, it surprised me she didn't draw blood. She didn't have the same faith in me as my uncle did, but she knew better than to defy him again. Her doubt made me want to prove myself harder. If my uncle thought I could do this, then I would show him I could.

"I can do whatever you need," I said because I didn't have a choice in the matter. If my uncle told me to do something, I was no different from anyone else he commanded. I had to do it.

"I want to trust Romero, but he's young and a bit of a hothead. I need to know what he's planning and intercede if necessary. I won't allow him to destroy all that I've accomplished."

"How long will I have to do this new job?"

"I can't answer that." My uncle stood and glanced at my aunt. "It will take as long as it takes."

How would I even get this information? Wouldn't that involve me spending time with Romero? I couldn't even sit a few feet away from him at a bar without trembling and cowering under his heavy stare. How was I going to get intel on him? If he was as cunning as I'd heard, wouldn't he see right through me?

"Romero is an interesting man," my aunt said. "Not at all easy to deal with. He has little patience and has a reputation for being cruel."

"What makes you think he'll tell me anything?" The more I thought about this, the more I realized I missed the bigger picture. "How am I supposed to get what you need if he doesn't trust me?"

"You'll gain his trust because he'll have no reason to doubt you." The certainty in his voice rattled me. "I'm putting you in a position that will guarantee you have access to everything I need."

"Why would he trust a paralegal?" I asked. "Especially one who works in your firm and is related to you?"

"This job is going to require a completely distinct skill set," my aunt said. "One I hope you have. You're not the most experienced woman around."

"All she has to do is be herself." My uncle motioned toward the door as my cousins filed in. "You said yourself, she already intrigued Romero."

"Every pretty face intrigues Romero." Vincent came into the office. "He's used to getting what he wants."

*Wait... did they expect me to give him...*

Sandro sat next to me. "Are you okay?"

"She's fine," my aunt answered for me.

Now that I saw the strange glances they gave one another, I was anything but fine. I pleaded with my eyes for Alessandro to help me, but he kept twisting that stupid, expensive tie between his fingers.

"Are we certain this is the best option?" Vincent asked. "Romero is a cruel bastard."

"We've gone over all our options." My uncle slammed

his palm into his desk, causing me to jump. "This is a done deal. Lu will serve her family because she's the only one who can right now. She will get us the information we need."

The room fell silent. No one dared to say anything.

"Are we clear?" My uncle yelled, his voice echoing through the office. I was certain the rest of the staff heard him, but since he lost his temper often, no one probably even worried.

I nodded. I was more confused now than I was before. I didn't know what they expected of me, and I was too afraid to ask.

"I won't be questioned by any of you. I know what's best for this family." He stared down at each one of us. "I always have. I provide for all of you. Not only will I leave a legacy when I'm gone, but the Torrio line will reap the benefits for generations to come."

"Well, in that case." Rocco ruffled my hair like he used to when I was a kid. His degrading action should have upset me, but the contact comforted me. "Congratulations are in order."

"Congratulations?" That was a strange thing to say. "Thanks, but the assignment is hardly a promotion."

"I'm not talking about any assignment." Rocco smiled at me. "I meant congratulations on your engagement, future Mrs. Bilotti."

Blood rushed to my head, and a chill coursed through me as my stomach churned. When I looked up, the most devious smirk crossed my aunt's blood-red lips.

*Going to the electric chair would have been a hell of a lot easier than this because being thrown to the wolf was so much more brutal.*

## CHAPTER 4

*Romero*

I took a few days to consider the alliance Giancarlo had presented to me. Joining forces with the Torrios made sense. With their connections and access to the ports in international waters, I could expand my business faster than even I could have imagined.

It was a lucrative opportunity, but it wasn't about the money. I already had plenty of that. It wasn't even about the power, because in time, I could gain that too. There was something else that called to me. A sweet and innocent woman who I could claim was a huge part of this transaction. That seemed to be the only element missing from my world these days.

I looked down at the fancy paper that I'd ripped out of the silver envelope a few minutes ago. They had delivered it via a messenger. I laughed at their audacity. Was this a joke to them?

"What's so amusing?" Gio entered my study.

"The almighty Torrios have invited me to my own

fucking engagement party with this expensive invitation. They didn't even send a family member to deliver it."

"Dude, that's cold."

"That's who they are." I threw the invitation onto my desk. I had the balls not to show up and leave that high and mighty family looking like a bunch of assholes in front of all their rich, snobby guests. "They've always thought they were better than us. Better than everyone else."

"And yet, we're joining them. I don't get it."

"Because you don't have the business sense I have. I can see the bigger picture. Do you know what their connections will do for us? This could set us up for life and never have to do the things Dad did to get to the top. We've found our own way. We don't need this organization or what it represents, but we will have their respect."

"If you say so." He shrugged. "You're the one who has to marry a Torrio."

At first, that condition was disturbing, especially after the way Antonio's wife negotiated the terms of the marriage. He took care of the business end of the alliance, but Kristina handled the portion where they handed over their niece to me. She was distant and calculated when she spoke of Luciana. She kept making it a point to tell me that once we married, Luciana was mine to do with as I pleased. As if I needed her aunt's permission to treat my wife any way I saw fit.

I had never considered myself the marrying type, and I certainly didn't expect to do it through an arranged deal. I'd almost told them to fuck off, but I had seen the exquisite Luciana Torrio in person last month at a reception. Her mere presence was enough to distract me from an important business negotiation that night. If I wasn't in the middle of a once in a lifetime offer, I would have told my associate to leave, and I would have pursued her.

I could tell when our eyes met, she wasn't sure she should even look at me. Her cheeks flushed a pretty pink, but it was her stunning gray eyes that caught my attention. I'd thought about her a few times, but because I knew who her family was, I didn't go any further with it. As fate would have it, the Torrios were handing her over to me, anyway.

"Once I marry his niece, he'll have to respect me."

"She's easy on the eyes, though," Gio said. "Isn't she a little young and inexperienced for you?"

"There's an age gap." My future bride was eleven years my junior, but that had never stopped me before. "Her inexperience is none of your business."

But it was going to be my business really soon.

"I'm sure you'll enjoy every pleasurable minute of it."

I smirked as I picked up the invitation and read it over. "I do admire the balls on Torrio for inviting me like this. He's showing me he's in control."

"What do you think she means to them if they could pawn her off on you?" Gio turned off the television and tossed the remote on the coffee table. "You're not the most respectable guy around."

"That's true." I poured myself a vodka from the bar on the marble counter behind my desk. "I would accuse them of pawning off a lowly family member, but she's the only one they have who could cement this union. If we move our shit through their territory, they'll benefit too. Aligning themselves with us gives them more guys in the field and more protection when they need it."

Luciana wasn't a true Torrio even though they'd raised her. I wasn't sure if that was a detriment or something I could use to my advantage later. Maybe if I wanted out of this alliance, I could say she wasn't worthy. Even without ever speaking to her, I already knew that wasn't true. I was probably the bastard who wasn't worthy of her. *Poor girl.* She was gaining me as a husband and if she was as pure as they promised me she was, she wouldn't be able to handle me.

*Fuck!* That made me hard thinking about it.

"In any case, this is a good deal." I sipped my drink. "If I have to go through the effort of getting married to make sure it happens, so be it."

I could act as if marrying her was a hardship, but I would gain a beautiful woman to not only stand by my side, but sleep in my bed and satisfy all of my needs. Who could say no to that?

"Why do you get all the fun sacrifices?" Gio asked.

"Because I'm the oldest."

"You may be the oldest, but I'm still the one dealing with Arturo."

It had been a few days, and we still had heard nothing from him. While his disappearance was alarming, it wasn't unusual in this business. I'd hate to think something had happened to him because he worked for me, but the possibility was there.

"Give it another day or two and then we'll figure it out."

No one had sent us a message telling us they had him. If he had gone underground, he would resurface soon. My client had received the shipment, so as of right now, I was the only one out of a lot of fucking money. If Arturo took off with my cash, there wouldn't be any place he could hide.

"I hope he's all right," Gio said. "He's a good guy. I'd hate to think we underestimated him and he turned on us."

"I'd be more concerned someone else got to him before I thought he betrayed us." I didn't often give people the benefit of the doubt, but I had good instincts. If I misread someone, I would use it to my advantage later. No one ever walked away from me unscathed.

"Maybe he's shacking up with some hottie and he'll resurface soon."

"Then I'll fucking kill him for making me sweat this out." I slammed my fist down on the desk.

"It's only money."

"A lot of fucking money." No way would Arturo be stupid enough to steal from me. "Let me know if you hear something."

"You'll be the first person I tell."

"What's the name of that boutique owner in the city? The one who has all the male clients who buy for their girlfriends, wives, and mistresses?"

"Kendall."

"Yeah, you've shopped with her before, right?"

"A few times."

"You were satisfied with her?"

"She hasn't let me down yet."

"I'm sure you've benefited on several occasions."

"I always get laid after I give a gift from her shop. She's not cheap, but you tell her exactly what you're looking for and your girl will look like a fucking runway model." He rested his head against the back of the sofa. "Do you know how much head I've gotten from women who appreciated the new wardrobes I bought for them?"

"Send me her number."

"Why?"

"Because my future bride will need a dress for our engagement party and I want to make sure she looks exactly the way I want her to. People will know she's mine before that night is over."

"I don't think you two have the same taste in clothing." Gio sent me Kendall's number.

"She's going to wear whatever I tell her to wear." I scrolled through my contacts until I came across Antonio Torrio's number. "I'm going to let them know we're coming."

"They can't have an engagement party without the groom."

"I guess they can't." I composed a text to my future in-law.

*Received your personal invitation. Very fancy. I'm RSPV'ing for me and my brother. You probably already guessed I'd be there.*

I hit send, but I had one more thing to add.

*I'm sending a gift to my fiancée. Make sure she receives it before the party.*

If Torrio and his little niece thought this arrangement was going to be easy, they had plenty to learn about me. The sooner everyone realized I was in charge, the better.

## CHAPTER 5

*Luciana*

The shiny, flat black box with the crimson *X* painted on top taunted me. A messenger had delivered it twenty minutes ago, but I still hadn't opened it. I was too nervous. I placed it on my bed, trying to figure out why Romero would send me anything at all.

Downstairs, the house bustled with chaos. The staff busied themselves preparing for my engagement party. Caterers, decorators, bartenders, and servers had been here all day, transforming the mansion into a beautiful display of white, twinkling lights, and hundreds of roses. If the engagement party was this extravagant, I couldn't imagine what the wedding would be like. All this work to throw a spectacular party and I hadn't even had a conversation with the man I was going to marry.

*It's business.* I kept telling myself that, but I'd been sick to my stomach ever since I'd agreed to this arrangement. Well, I didn't really agree to it, which was probably why my stomach was so upset. I had done a few internet searches on my future husband, and I didn't like anything I read about him. Of course, one couldn't believe everything they read on the internet, but something told me most of what I found was true.

The red *X* was Romero's mark. According a local reporter, it symbolized his rise to the top. When his father died, he walked away from the family business with nothing. He started from the bottom, clawing his way to the top and doing unspeakable things to get where he was today. Now, he needed the Torrio family to continue that rise, and I was his key to getting what he wanted. Only, this was a set-up, and I was the bait.

I traced my finger along the *X* on the package. He had already agreed to marry me. Would he do that and send a package to blow me up? According to some things I'd read about him, that was exactly what he'd do.

Alessandro barged into my room. He sat on my bed, lifting the box onto his lap. "What's this? It's very chic."

"A gift from Romero." I sat next to him. "It was delivered a few minutes ago."

"Aren't you going to open it?"

"I don't know."

"You don't know?"

"What if it's a bomb or something?"

"Why would he send you a bomb?" He ripped open the lid with no qualms about being blown to smithereens. "Here."

He handed me a black envelope with my name written in silver.

"Thanks." I opened the envelope and took out the paper inside while Alessandro pulled out a red, silky fabric from the box. He mumbled something about it being way too sexy for me. I ignored his comment as I read the note.

*Luciana,*

*Meet me outside at 9:00 pm and we'll go into the party together. Wear this dress for me.*

*R*

He wanted us to go in together. It wasn't an outrageous request, considering everyone in attendance would be there to celebrate our engagement. But I couldn't get over me not knowing him. How were we supposed to make an entrance and look like a couple who not only was engaged but who were going to get married? Did everyone already believe this charade?

Sandro stood and held the dress up for me to see. It was incredible. Slinky, crimson, and sexier than anything I owned. Totally not me.

"I can't wear that."

"Why not?" He looked me over. "You have the body for it."

"That's gross."

"Come on, Lu. I'm allowed to say you're a gorgeous woman even though I know you don't believe it."

"I'll look ridiculous in that dress." I ran the expensive fabric through my fingers. If I did wear it, I'd feel like a woman. "It's not at all my style."

"Your style might have to change once Bilotti becomes your husband."

"I'm not changing who I am for him." I got up and paced the room. "This is an assignment. I'm only doing this to help your dad. It's a part I have to play until I can figure a way out of it."

"What if there isn't a way out of it?"

"Why would you say that?"

"Do you honestly believe my father would go through all of this if he didn't want you in it for the long haul?" He set the dress on my bed. "Why are you so naïve?"

"I'm not." I liked being in the dark with the family business. The less I knew, the better off I was. That was all going to change once I walked into that party with Romero. My innocence would be lost. "I agreed to help."

"You didn't have a choice. None of us do."

"What are you saying? Do you think I'm going to stay married to a man I don't even know? I'm going to get what your dad needs and I'm going to walk away."

"I hope you're right."

"Don't you ever dream about being free from all this? You're different from Vincent and Rocco. I've always known that."

"I'm a Torrio."

"That doesn't mean you can't be your own person."

"Soon you're going to be a Bilotti and you're going to understand what that means." He took my hand. "Be strong."

"You're scaring me."

"Good." He stared into my eyes. "You're making a tremendous sacrifice tonight. We won't forget what you're doing for us, but you have to be careful. What my dad is asking you to do is dangerous. If Bilotti realizes this is a trap...be careful, okay?"

"I'm going to be fine." I didn't exactly believe that, but I'd never seen Sandro so serious before. I wanted to ease his mind but knowing that my uncle was willingly marrying me to a potential enemy didn't sit well with me. "I can do this."

"I believe you can, Lu." He hugged me. "Believe you can, too."

"I'm going to miss you, so promise you'll come visit me when I have to leave here to live with him." My eyes filled with tears as I held onto him.

"All you have to do is call and I'll be there." He let go of me. "You're not going to have to do this alone."

"This conversation is far too serious." I wiped the tears from my cheeks. "This is supposed to be a happy night, right?"

"That's why I came in here." He reached into his inside suit jacket pocket and handed me a satin bag. "I have a gift for you."

"What is it?" I took the soft purple bag from him. "You didn't have to get me anything."

"You might need what's inside there."

I pulled apart the pouch and spilled the contents onto the bed. I crinkled my nose as I studied the odd gifts: a black garter belt, a small knife, and a condom packet. "Are you serious?"

"Dealer's choice." He smirked. "You never know how the night will go."

"Get out of here!" I threw a pillow at him on his way out. "I have to get ready."

~

I MADE my way down the back staircase and through the hectic kitchen. Servers popped bottles of champagne and poured it into delicate crystal glasses. The chefs my aunt had brought in for the occasion were carefully plating appetizers and placing them on trays. No one noticed me as I slipped by them and went out the back door.

It was ten after nine. I would have been on time, but I decided the dress Romero sent me was too over the top. I changed into my favorite black dress instead. I hoped I didn't offend my future husband by not wearing his gift. Maybe we could go to dinner another time and I could wear it then. I was too nervous tonight and didn't want to have to worry about my boobs popping out of the slinky dress he'd sent.

I made my way through the backyard as the cool April breeze swept along my skin. When I trembled, I realized it was more about being anxious than it was about the nighttime spring air.

Sandro's words weighed heavily on me. It bothered me that no one could give me a timetable for this charade. How long would they expect me to stay married to a man who I knew nothing about? A month, six months, a year? A year seemed like such a long time. How much information would my uncle need before he realized he could either trust Romero or not? Once he got what he needed, would Romero let me walk away? Why hadn't I asked these questions before I'd agreed to this? Maybe I had. Everything was a blur.

I opened the side gate and gazed down the path that led to the main driveway. Torrio guards were patrolling the property. I smiled and waved to a couple as I headed toward some parked cars, spying two men in the distance. When I realized one of them was Romero, I stopped in my tracks.

The house and landscape lights allowed me to get a good look at him. I'd seen him that one time in person but only for a few minutes, and in some pictures online, but now he seemed more intimidating to me. A scowl crossed his face when he checked his watch, but it didn't take away from his stunning features. A light stubble covered his sculpted jaw. The back of his dark hair was cropped close to his head, but the front was longer and tousled neatly with some kind of styling product.

I willed my feet to move closer, so I could get a better look at the man I was going to marry. He wore a black suit, with a black shirt, and a red tie. I swallowed hard. Did he match the tie to the dress he had given me? He was an imposing figure at over six feet tall. His chest was broad and his arms were all muscle.

I brushed against the trees, making a slight noise. Romero's head snapped in my direction, his enchanting green eyes locked with mine. I stood frozen, afraid to go to him. An awkward sensation hit me. We were about to create a memory. Most couples had funny stories of when they dated, memorable first kisses, and unforgettable proposals. All we would have was a brief meeting before walking into a party and making a room full of strangers believe we were a couple.

When I finally got the nerve to move, he leaned against his sleek, black SUV and whispered something to the man he was with. As I got closer, I recognized him as Romero's brother, Gio. He disappeared toward the house when I approached. I stopped a few feet from Romero, allowing myself to get lost in his hard gaze as I shuffled my feet and clasped my hands together to keep from fidgeting.

"You're late." He moved towards me "You're going to have to learn real quick that my time is very important and I don't tolerate disrespect."

*Wow! So much for a cute, memorable first meeting. Jerk!*

**CHAPTER 6**

*Romero*

I glanced at my watch for the fourth time since we got to the Torrio estate. She was late. I hated when people were late. Who the hell did she think she was making me stand outside like a friggin' commoner waiting for her? As each second passed, the more infuriated I became. What could be more important than her being on time for her own engagement party?

"Look at these guards staring at us." I nodded toward the muscle paid to protect the Torrio estate. "Even they think they're better than us. I wonder if they'd feel that way if I blew one of their heads off?"

"Could you relax for five minutes?" Gio shoved his phone in his pocket. "This is supposed to be a celebration."

"Maybe it would be if my fiancée could manage to tell time."

"She's only ten minutes late." He laughed. "That's what women do. They keep us waiting."

"Not my woman."

"You have a lot to learn." He snickered. "You won't be able to treat your wife the way you do your associates."

"Watch me."

"You're on edge." He handed me his flask. "Drink this."

"I should keep my wits about me."

"A little is not going to hurt," my brother encouraged me.

I took a long sip of the smooth vodka from the silver container, letting it coat my throat. "What if these people try something?"

"With a house full of associates? That would be really stupid of them."

"You never know. They could all be in cahoots for all we know." I motioned to the car behind us, occupied by my security team. "Make sure they stay alert."

"The Torrios are welcoming you into their family. Why would they go through all this trouble to kill you?"

"They wouldn't." I took another swig from the flask before handing it back to him. "I won't settle down until the marriage certificate is signed. That will bind the two families and strengthen our position."

A rustling in the bushes caught my attention. When I looked in the direction of the backyard, Luciana stepped out, but stopped when our eyes met.

*Fuck!* She was absolutely stunning. She was a beautiful woman but seeing her tonight gave me a whole new perspective. Her black, shiny hair flowed over her shoulders and curled at the ends. Her toned legs seem to go on forever.

How long would I have to wait to have them wrapped around me?

As she approached, the only flaw I could find with my

goddess was she wasn't wearing the dress I'd sent her. Why would she disrespect me like that?

"Wow," Gio whispered. "She's amazing."

"She's defiant," I hissed as I tried to contain my anger. "Go to her room and get the dress I sent her."

"Are you sure that's what you want me to do? The one she has on is perfect."

"I wouldn't have fucking asked you to do it if I wasn't sure."

"Fine." He left without arguing.

Luciana made her way to me, stopping more than an arm's length. That wouldn't do.

"You're late." I moved closer to her. "You're going to have to learn real quick that my time is very important and I don't tolerate disrespect."

"I'm sorry." She shuffled her feet. "I was getting ready, and I lost track of time."

"I won't deny that you look beautiful, Luciana, but why aren't you wearing the dress I sent?"

I took in the way the black dress hugged her subtle curves and clung to her perky breasts. The dress she had chosen was classy and suited her, but I wanted her to wear the one I gave her.

"Thank you for the gift."

At least she was polite in her rejection.

"I liked the one you sent me but it's not my style." She wriggled her hands. "I'm really nervous about tonight and I didn't feel comfortable in it. I thought I could wear it when it was just the two of us."

That was a reasonable explanation, but it didn't satisfy me. I had requested she do something for me and she refused. We weren't off to a great start.

"You've insulted me twice tonight, Luciana." I inched

closer to her until there was no space between us. When she backed away, I reached for her, wrapping my arm around her waist and holding her against me.

Her cheeks flushed that alluring shade of pink. Was that what her ass cheeks would look like after I spanked the shit out of her? She appeared uncomfortable, but she was going to have to get used to me touching her. I planned on doing it a lot.

"First, you were late, and then you refused my gift. Is that anyway to start our engagement?"

She looked up at me with fear in her wide, gray eyes.

"I'm sorry," she mumbled. "I didn't mean to offend you."

I lowered my gaze to her glossy, full lips, licking mine when I thought about kissing her.

"You can call me Lu," she said.

"What?" Her ridiculous statement distracted me from her mouth.

"You keep calling me Luciana but no one does."

"Isn't that your name?"

"Everyone calls me Lu."

"The sooner you realize I'm not like everyone else, *Luciana,* the better off you'll be."

"Why did you agree to this?" She dropped her gaze. "Why do you want to marry me?"

"Because it benefits me and I always do what benefits me."

"So, it's just business for you?"

What did she want me to say? Yes, it was business, but it didn't hurt that she was the prize. If I could find some pleasure in this whole arrangement, would that be so bad? If we had to get married, we should enjoy it.

"What is this about for you?" I asked. "I know why I agreed, but why would you?"

The answer was obvious with a family like hers, but I wanted to hear her say it.

"I, um, I didn't have a choice." Her voice was soft and laced with regret, but I admired her honesty. "It doesn't matter. I've agreed and here we are."

*Did she have to look so fucking sad?*

"We should probably go inside now," she said. "They're waiting for us."

"We'll go inside after you change."

"Change what?" Her cute little nose crinkled.

"Did you get it?" I asked my brother as he approached us.

"Here." He handed me the dress as he spoke to her. "You must be Luciana."

She nodded as she stared at the dress in my hands. Her eyes filled with tears when she realized what Gio had given me, but she quickly wiped them away.

"This is my brother Gio," I said. "We'll meet you in the house in a few minutes."

"Okay." Gio walked away because he knew better than to defy me. I hoped Luciana would follow his lead and do what I said. I wasn't in the mood to fight with her.

I opened the back passenger door of my SUV. "Get in."

"Why?"

"Because I said so." I grabbed her by the elbow and shoved her into the car. "Put this on. Now."

I tossed the dress at her. I got into the back seat with her and slammed the door.

"I already told you I'm not wearing this." She threw the dress at me, igniting a rage from deep within me.

*You shouldn't have gone there, sweetheart.*

"Maybe you didn't understand when I said I wouldn't tolerate your disrespect." I moved close to her, pushing her down and getting on top of her. I pinned her against the leather seat with the weight of my body.

"Get off me!" She pushed against my chest, but she was no match for me. "Stop it!"

Her struggles only fueled my fire. The more she fought me, the more aroused I became. She had no idea how much I liked a good fight. If she kept this up, I would fuck her right here.

I grasped the front of her dress in my firm grip and ripped it down the center, revealing her black strapless bra and matching panties. She trembled under my gaze, the embarrassment evident in her eyes, but I couldn't stop staring at her breasts as they spilled out of the top of her bra. Her stomach was flat and cut with muscles. *Sweet.* Her panties were tiny and barely covered her pussy. They were revealing enough for me to see she had waxed. Did she do that for me?

"Please." She breathed hard against me.

"Please what?" I traced my finger along her throat and down her chest, swirling it over her nipple. "You caused this situation. I'm just correcting it."

"You're an asshole."

"Tell me something I don't know." I circled my finger around her other nipple. "Your family gave you to me, Luciana."

She shook her head as if I wasn't speaking the truth.

"All of you." I trailed my hand down her smooth stomach and to the edge of her panties, sliding my finger inside them.

"No." She wiggled beneath me, stirring against my erection.

"So, when you ask me if this is just business, the answer is yes." I pressed my lips to the throbbing vein on her neck.

"But that doesn't mean I won't claim every glorious inch of you and there isn't anything you can do about it."

I got off her and threw the dress at her. "Wear this or your underwear. I don't care, but now we're late and that reflects on me."

She huffed as she tugged the dress over her head, trying to cover her breasts, but it dipped low, revealing a lovely amount of cleavage.

"That's better," I said. "If you would have worn it in the first place, we could already be inside. As much as I like this game we're playing, now is not the time."

"It's really messed up that your brother knew where my room was."

We were aware of the whole layout of the mansion. I liked to be prepared for situations like tonight. If I needed an escape route, I didn't want to be caught in uncertain circumstances.

Once she was dressed, I opened the door and got out of the car. She slid toward me, so I reached for her to help her out. She swatted my hand away and got out on her own. When her feet hit the ground, she straightened the dress over her thighs and fixed her hair.

"You look fine."

"I don't need your approval." She walked ahead of me, giving me a delightful view of her sexy ass.

*Feisty little thing.* Too bad it was all an act.

I reached into my pants pocket and took out the one thing we definitely needed if we were going to be engaged. I hurried my pace, catching up to her and grabbing her hand. When she tried to pull away, I held her wrist tighter. When would she stop defying me?

"Why do you have to be so fucking stubborn?" I took her hand in mine and slipped the impressive diamond engagement ring on her finger. "We can't exactly have an engagement without this."

She stared down at the shiny ring. Did she like it? Was that her style? I didn't know many women who would refuse such a spectacular piece of jewelry. Although, I had a feeling Luciana Torrio was nothing like any woman I'd ever encountered before. Maybe that was why she intrigued me.

"It's spectacular," she whispered. "I didn't expect...I mean, I didn't think you would have a ring."

"It was my mother's. It was left to me after she... I inherited it." I willed myself not to think about my mother. Not now, not today.

"I'm not stubborn," she said as we entered the house. "I'm just nervous."

"Nervous?" I straightened my posture as we made our way through the foyer. "You're not the one these people look down on. None of them can believe I made it this far. They all thought I'd be dead by the time I was twenty. I still don't have their respect, but that's about to change."

"Is it really that important? Why does someone as powerful as you care what these people think? You don't strike me as a man who needs anyone."

"You don't know much about the world you grew up in, do you?"

"I was fine with not knowing anything about it, but now I'm being thrown in the middle of it all and I'm not sure about any of it."

"Buckle up, baby, because your entire world is about to change forever."

"That's what I'm afraid of."

**CHAPTER 7**

*Luciana*

The barbarian gave me his dead mother's ring? Why did that make me feel bad? I stared down at my finger, admiring the large princess cut diamond set in the white gold band. I'd never owned such a magnificent piece of jewelry. A part of me couldn't help but gloat when I realized it was way bigger than my aunt's ring.

Before he'd put that ring on my finger, I was ready to make a run for it. *I still am.* But the sincerity in his voice when he told me it belonged to his mother tugged at my heartstrings.

When we walked through the living room and onto the back patio, my uncle introduced us to the waiting crowd. Everyone stared at us. A few applauded. Some women shot daggers in my direction. *Seriously?* They could have Romero. I'd gladly step aside, especially after the way he had treated me over the dress.

"The future Mr. and Mrs. Bilotti." Uncle Antonio raised a glass of champagne to us as a server handed each of us a crystal flute. "Tonight is a monumental occasion for the Torrio and Bilotti families. With the engagement of my niece to Romero, we join two powerful entities."

The pride in my uncle's words made me want to vomit. This was nothing more than a lucrative deal that worked for him either way. I would spy for as long as it took, and if I found incriminating evidence, my uncle would win. If Romero was true to his word and he wasn't betraying the Torrios, my uncle gained again. The only one in this scenario who lost was yours truly.

"Once this alliance is realized, there will be no stopping us," my uncle continued. "Welcome to the Torrio family, Romero."

Romero possessively put his arm around my waist, lowering his lips to my ear. "Your uncle just gave you to me."

A shiver ran down my spine. Romero thought I was a possession.

"To Romero and Luciana," my uncle said. "May you both enjoy a happy and long future as husband and wife."

*Long?*

"Thank you." Romero guided me forward. "My brother Gio and I are honored to join forces with your family."

He held me closer, placing his hand on my backside.

When everyone stared at us, an uncomfortable awareness came over me. Romero wondered why my family looked down on him, but how could they not when he acted like a neanderthal. I tried to create some distance between us, but he wasn't having it. When he shot me a warning glare, I stopped moving.

"You've trusted me with a valuable member of your family, and I intend to treat her just as you have."

*Well, that's not good.* I glanced at my aunt as she took

pleasure in this arrangement. Did this mean I was trading one house for another that was even worse? I turned and stared at my future husband, listening as he spoke about alliances and making the two families stronger, and how in the long run, it would make all the families successful. He sounded as if he knew what he was talking about. His words were careful and his speech articulate, almost as if he had some education hidden beneath that rough exterior of his. Was that an act?

"To my fiancée." He raised his glass to me. "I promise to cherish and protect you for the rest of our lives."

With a shaky hand, I raised my flute and clinked it to his. *The rest of our lives?* That seemed like a really long time. Before I had time to process his words, he ushered me across the backyard and to the gazebo. Everyone raised their glasses to us when we passed them.

"Your family spared no expense for this sham." He gazed out at the band playing in the distance. "They're extremely ostentatious."

"It didn't stop you from coming here and collecting what they offered, did it?"

"No." He smirked. "But what man in his right mind would pass up the opportunity to marry you?"

"Was that supposed to be a compliment?"

"Take it however you'd like." He set his flute down, on the floor of the gazebo then took mine from me and placed it next to his. "I see you're still upset about the wardrobe change."

"You treated me like a possession. Like I don't matter."

"If you want me to treat you differently, you'll need to change your attitude."

"I'm not changing for you. Not my clothes, not my attitude, not who I am." I crossed my arms over my chest like a petulant child, but I didn't care. I had to get my point across.

"Do you even know who you are? How can you expect me to if you have no idea?"

I rolled my eyes at him and called him an ass under my breath.

"Do you know what happens to little girls who act like brats?" He grabbed my forearms and tugged me to him. "They get treated like brats. Are you sure you want to test me?"

"I'm not afraid of you." If I wasn't trembling so hard, he might have believed me.

"I don't tolerate liars, Luciana."

"I'm learning you don't tolerate a lot of things."

"Good."

When I tried to struggle out of his hold, he held me tighter, clasping one hand in mine and wrapping his arm around my waist.

"What are you doing?" I asked.

"Dancing with my future wife." When he brushed his lips along my jaw, I wanted to smack him, but I held still and let him do what he wanted. "We should look the part, don't you think?"

"I didn't ask to play this part."

"Neither did I, my little butterfly, but here we are." He spun us in a slow circle, locking his gaze with mine. "This entire set-up isn't ideal for me either, but it needs to be done."

"I don't understand why." That wasn't entirely true. I understood my role in all of this. I was a spy for the Torrio family, so I got why I had to marry him. The part that perplexed me was why did he agree to marry me? Was gaining access to a territory and joining two powerful families together that important?

"You'll get it, eventually." He held me against him. "Right now, you have to follow my lead and do what I say and you might gain some pleasure out of all of this."

"I doubt that," I mumbled.

"Well, I certainly plan to gain a lot of pleasure from you." He cupped my chin in his hand, hard enough to leave finger marks on my face. "I'm going to own your pleasure, too. You'll be begging me for it."

"You're disgusting."

"Am I?" He closed the small space between us, pressing his erection against my stomach. "Do you find that disgusting too, my innocent brat?"

"Stop it."

"This might be an inconvenient arrangement, but it won't be without its benefits. Once you're in my house, Luciana, in my bed, you'll understand why I agreed to this."

"What if I don't comply?"

"Do I look like the type of man who cares if you comply or not?" He gripped my chin harder. "Once you say *I do,* you're mine. If you don't think you can handle all that comes with being my wife, it's best you back out now."

"You know I can't do that."

"Then play nice." He dipped his head, focusing on my mouth. "I don't have the patience for your defiance."

When his breath danced across my lips, a shiver swept down my spine. Not because I was afraid or cold. It was something else. Something I couldn't understand. Something I didn't want to understand.

*God, what's wrong with me?*

"There you are," my uncle said.

When Romero released me, I stepped back, never so happy to see my aunt and uncle as I was at that moment.

Romero was far too intense for me. How was I going to marry him and expect to survive?

"Romero." Uncle Antonio motioned toward the house. "I'd like to finalize a few things with you."

"Of course." Romero stared at me. "Will you excuse me?"

I nodded.

When he took my hand and grazed his lips along my knuckles, all the warning bells blared between my ears. I was the prey caught in the wolf's trap, and my pack wouldn't save me.

The men walked away, but my aunt stayed behind, taking a seat on the bench under the gazebo.

"He's a wild one." She lit her cigarette. Her smoking habit had been a point of contention between her and my uncle for years. He finally allowed her to do it as long as it was outside and out of his sight. "Far too feral for you."

"He's not that bad." He was far worse, but I wouldn't let her know how scared I was.

"I noticed the dress you're wearing isn't the one you planned to wear this evening." She took a drag of her cigarette. "It's not the one you were wearing when you left your room either."

"It was a gift from Romero." I glanced down at the dress that had caused such an issue this evening. Who would have thought an eight-hundred-dollar piece of silk would create such havoc? "There was a misunderstanding, but we resolved it."

"That's what marriage is all about, isn't it? The give and the take."

"I wouldn't know." I turned to face the party, noting how many people I'd never met came out to celebrate my fake engagement. "I've never been married."

"You're going to find out soon enough that you'll be

doing a lot more giving than you will take, especially with a man like Bilotti. He's heartless and won't care about your feelings." She joined me at the edge of the gazebo. "Which is why you cannot get caught. If he finds out you're spying for us, he'll slit your throat without a second thought."

"Why are you bothering to tell me any of this? It's not like you care what happens to me."

"You're right, Lu, I don't care what happens to you, but my husband does to some degree, and I know my boys do. If you screw this up, they will never forgive themselves."

"Do you have any advice for me not to screw this up?" Would it kill her to assist me in helping her family?

"Keep your head down and act like you don't have any interest in his business. Observe everything, but don't ask him too many questions. He'll become suspicious of you and your motives." She dropped her cigarette on the ground and put it out with the toe of her stiletto. "Get as much information as you can. Report back everything, even if you don't think it's important."

"I don't even know what I'm looking for."

"You'll figure it out."

"Are you sure there's no other way to get what you need?" I didn't want to do this. Romero and I already had a toxic relationship, and we'd only known each other for an hour. "I can't be your best option."

"You're not."

"Then why are you doing this to me?"

None of this made any sense. If they trusted me so little, why would they give me such a crucial job? If Romero was as cunning as everyone made him out to be, wouldn't he figure out our plan before it even got started?

"You're the only option." She stepped out of the gazebo.

"Let's hope you're more like your uncle and less like your mother."

"What's that supposed to mean?"

"It means don't get yourself killed, and you better not get any of my family killed." She glared at me with her cold eyes. "Or I promise you, there will be nowhere for you to hide."

## CHAPTER 8

*Romero*

Leaving Luciana with that witch didn't sit well with me. There was something about Kristina Torrio I didn't like. If she and her husband hadn't interrupted me, I might have been in Luciana's room right now, taking what belonged to me.

No, I had to be strong and hold out until our wedding night. My fiancée tried to play a big game, but she was afraid of me, and she definitely didn't trust me. I'd have to show her what it meant to be my wife.

Gio huddled in a corner by the pool, surrounded by three women. I waved him over. He left his new entourage and followed me into the house and to Antonio's study. I'd never take a meeting this crucial without my second.

Vincent, Rocco, and Alessandro were all waiting for us. None of them said anything, but they all stared me down.

Please, these *lawyers* were no match for me. I took a seat that wasn't offered in the chair by the door.

"Giancarlo has approved all the terms, as I'm sure he told you." Antonio handed me the contracts that outlined all our *legitimate* dealings. The illegal shit would have to stand on the honor system, as we would put nothing like that in writing. I read everything carefully, before handing it to Gio so he could be a second set of eyes. I wouldn't put it past this family to cheat us out of something.

"Everything looks in order." Gio gave the papers back to me.

I signed the appropriate lines. "I want copies sent to me in the morning."

"Rocco will take care of that," Antonio said. "You'll have them first thing."

"Thank you." I leaned back in my chair. "I trust you're taking care of all the wedding plans?"

"My wife is handling all of that but I can assure you, it will be perfect."

"How is Luciana handling all of this?" I asked. "Do you think she'll go through with it?"

"Does she have a choice?" Vincent snapped. "We're not going to go back on our end of the deal."

"I didn't say you would, but your cousin is a little skittish around me." Images of her frightened eyes as I ripped that black dress from her crossed my mind.

"Can you blame her?" The youngest sibling challenged me.

"Sandro," Vincent said. "We've been through this. Romero marrying Lu makes the most sense for both families."

"It doesn't make much sense for Lu though, does it?" Alessandro glared at me. "You better not hurt her."

"Is that a threat?" Gio stepped toward him. "Because it's my job to handle those."

"That's enough," Antonio said. "Romero, you don't have

to worry about Lu. She will marry you and she won't give you any trouble."

*Somehow, I doubt that.*

"Once you're married, she's your responsibility," Antonio said. "We will no longer employ her at the firm. It's best that she makes a life with you."

"Dependent on him," Sandro mumbled.

"She won't need that measly job." I looked at Alessandro. "I'll provide for her."

"She isn't the type of woman who will sit around all day and do nothing. She has hopes and dreams. Luciana wants to be…" Sandro stopped. "Lu isn't the desperate housewife type."

"She's going to be any type I want her to be," I said.

Rocco stood in the corner, the only one of the clan yet to speak. I'd heard he was the brains of the operation. He was cold and calculated but he had a soft spot for my future bride. Judging from the way he eyed me up, he didn't approve of me.

Antonio poured each of us a glass of scotch from an elaborate crystal decanter on his desk and gave them to us. I guessed this was the part where we bonded over our new alliance and celebrated my engagement to their treasured family member. The problem was, if she was so important, why would they hand her over to me? It was obvious none of them trusted me.

"Is there anything else you want to know before the wedding?" Antonio asked. "I'm sure between the four of us, we can answer any questions you have about Lu."

"I can ask her what I need to know." I should have left it there, but the smug, 'I'm better than you,' smirks on their faces pissed me off. "There is one thing and depending on your answer, it could be a deal breaker."

"What would that be?" Antonio asked.

"Is your precious niece a virgin?"

"Are you fucking kidding me?" Rocco stepped forward. "How crude could you be?"

"He speaks." When I stood to meet him, Gio moved with me. "I don't think it's an unreasonable question."

"It's a disrespectful question," Rocco said. "Why would you ask us about that? Are you trying to humiliate Lu?"

"Rocco." Antonio held up his hand. "If this conversation is too much for you, you may leave."

"I'll stay." Rocco gritted his teeth. "Someone has to look out for her."

"I believe my niece is pure," Antonio assured me. "Of course, I can't guarantee it, as I'm not with her every second of her life. She hasn't had a serious boyfriend."

"Most guys are afraid of us," Vincent said. "This is a conversation you should have with her."

"I intend to." I finished my drink. "If we're done here, I'd like to get back to my fiancée."

"There's one other thing," Antonio said. "This may be an arrangement between us, but Lu is not expendable. I expect you to treat her well."

His request took me by surprise. I thought they considered her quite expendable, especially after the way her aunt negotiated the marriage deal. She basically told me Luciana would be mine to do as I pleased. She said she knew my reputation wasn't stellar and her niece could benefit from a strong, dominant man to put her in her place. I figured Luciana was some spoiled, out-of-control girl, but now I wasn't so sure.

Kristina Torrio had put herself on my radar. Most people tried to stay out of my way. But after having this conversation with her husband and sons, I was more certain than ever that she had an agenda. I needed to figure out why it included my future wife.

Gio and I left the study, shutting the door behind us so the Torrios could talk about us.

"That went well." Gio took out his flask. "It's empty. Let's get a drink."

"You go." I glanced around the crowded house. "I want to find Luciana and say goodnight."

"Are you sure that's a good idea?"

"Why wouldn't it be?"

"Your bride didn't look like she was that comfortable around you. Maybe you should consider small doses until the wedding. You don't want to give her a reason to run."

"She won't run."

Tonight had been an enlightening experience. Luciana may have acted like she didn't want to be with me, but her life here wasn't perfect. These people may have taken her in when she was a child, but I didn't get the vibe that they totally embraced her. I could get her away from these people if that was what she wanted. The concerning part was, why did I care?

"I'll be at the bar," Gio said.

"I'll meet you there in twenty minutes." I made my way through the hordes of people who were here to celebrate my engagement to Luciana. Most of them didn't care that I was marrying a Torrio. All they concerned themselves with was how I could advance their position. Some of them were going to be disappointed since I had little use for them. Once I married in to this family and had the Torrio network, I'd work my way through the list and see who was worth my time and who could fuck off.

As I came through the kitchen, something told me Luciana wasn't outside. I made my way up the back staircase and to her bedroom. It was down a long hall and set away from the other bedrooms. Had she been isolated her entire life? The hallway was dimly lit, but I found her door without incident.

I reached for the handle but hesitated. Should I knock? *Fuck no. Why would I?* I turned the handle and entered the room.

"What the hell?" Luciana screamed from the bed. "What are you doing in here?"

"Looking for you." I came into the bedroom and closed the door. "What are you doing up here?"

"Nothing." She slipped off the bed and set the glass of wine she had been sipping when I came in on the end table beside her. "I had enough of the party."

She still wore the dress, but she'd taken off her shoes, leaving her delicate feet bare. Her perfectly pedicured silver toenails sparkled and there was a small heart tattoo on the inside of her right ankle.

"How did the meeting with my uncle go?"

"Uneventful." I moved closer to her, but she backed away.

"Don't do that."

"Do what?"

"Retreat when I come near you." I closed the space between us. "I don't like it."

"It's instinctual."

"Have you been crying?" I ran my thumb under her eye, wiping away her smeared mascara.

"No."

"What did I tell you about lying?"

"Would you really care if I was crying?" She sat on the edge of the bed. "You're like everyone else around here. You don't care what I want or what I need."

"You're wrong." I leaned against the door because I didn't trust myself to sit on the bed with her. I'd want to touch her, and touching would lead to kissing, and kissing would lead to fucking. "I'm not like anyone around here."

"Whatever."

I clenched my fist by my side, trying to keep my anger in check. If I unleashed on her now, I'd never gain her trust, but I wouldn't allow her to disrespect me.

"Watch your tone." I kept the distance between us. "I don't want to have to put you in your place tonight."

"You can go now," she said.

"Are you dismissing me?" I laughed because no one had ever spoken to me like that before.

"I've had my fill of you tonight."

"I realize this is overwhelming for you." I broke my rule and closed the distance between us, standing in front of her. "We're both going to have to adjust, so I suggest you do better or I'll make you regret it."

"Don't threaten me."

"Threaten you?" I twisted my fingers in her hair and yanked her head forward. "Don't underestimate the control I'm exercising right now."

I tightened my grip on her hair, making her whimper. "I don't threaten."

"Let go of me." She struggled against my hold, but I jerked at her hair, forcing her to stay still.

She had no idea what her resistance stirred inside me.

"What I really want to do is force you on your knees, shove my cock in that defiant mouth of yours, and cum down your throat."

She gasped.

"Don't push me." I released her hair and stepped back. "I'm not a forgiving man but I'll allow you tonight to figure things out. I don't want to go into this marriage constantly fighting you. It'll be up to you how we proceed."

She didn't speak, and that was probably the best thing she could have done. I didn't know how much more control I had when it came to her. This wedding couldn't come fast enough. Two weeks until I could sink my cock into her innocent body. Would I make it that long?

"I'll be in touch. Sweet dreams, butterfly." I left the bedroom, closing the door behind me.

As I strolled down the hall, the sound of glass shattered against the other side of her bedroom door.

*My girl has some spunk.*

**CHAPTER 9**

*Luciana*

A few days after the party, I discovered a small package wrapped in black paper with the prominent red X displayed on top. It taunted me from the spare pillow next to my head. Romero and Gio may have had free access to the house during the party the other night, but there was no way either of them could have strolled in here and left a present for me without security noticing. *Could they?*

I sat up and placed the box in my lap. Would he blow me up this time? *Probably not.* I ripped the paper off and lifted the lid. The contents didn't seem threatening. I took out a set of keys and a note with my name on it.

*Luciana,*

*Meet me at 223 North Haven Road at 1 pm. Don't be late or there will be consequences.*

*R*

I held the set of keys in my hand. What were they for? I reached for my phone and searched for the address. The house was in a secluded neighborhood in New Jersey, about thirty minutes from the city. It wasn't far from where I currently lived. Whose house was on North Haven Road? Why did he want to meet me there?

We hadn't spoken since the night of the party. It relieved part of me that I didn't have to deal with his intimidating personality. The other part, the part that I doubted the sanity of, missed him. I couldn't stop thinking about his erection when we danced. How he'd threatened to shove his cock in my mouth. I should have been repulsed and I pretended I was, but that wasn't true. His rough mannerisms, how he handled me and spoke to me, excited me. I didn't know what to do with that.

His dominating personality terrified me, but his physical form frightened me even more. I'd never been with a man like him before. I'd dated boys in high school and one or two in college, but nothing serious. No one I had ever been interested in looked like him. Muscles, tattoos, expensive designer suits. His solid body had been on my mind since he'd tossed me in the back of his SUV and ripped my dress from me. He was firm, powerful, and hard. So hard.

*What is wrong with me?* He was a caveman. I'd read enough romance novels to know that the way he handled me was not the way it was supposed to be. He wanted to own me. That was sick and twisted. This entire situation was wrong. None of it was how it should be. My family forced me to agree to marry him. He had no intention of making any of this easy for me. I had to figure out how to be his wife, do what my family wanted, and not get killed in the process.

*Easier said than done.*

After I showered, blew out my hair, and did my makeup to perfection, I raided my closet. I wanted to look good, but this time, the outfit would be my choice. Why was I going through all this trouble? Did I care what he thought about me?

*Yes, too much.*

After tossing five or six outfits on the floor, I found the one I wanted: a white strapless dress with a short black leather jacket to go over it. For the finishing touch on the ensemble, red, open-toed strappy heels. He seemed to like red.

Was the outfit over the top for an afternoon meeting? *Probably.* Would it be enough to tempt my future husband? *Hopefully.*

I wasn't sure why I wanted to provoke him like this, but why not?

I grabbed my bag from my vanity chair and hurried down the stairs and through the foyer. I didn't want to be late this time. Romero didn't seem like the type of guy who would let that go a second time. I dug my keys out of my purse and darted for the door.

"Lu." Rocco came out of my uncle's study. "Where are you headed in such a rush?"

"Uh, I'm meeting Romero."

"I want to talk to you."

"Can it wait until tonight? I don't want to be late." Did that sound too eager? "I'm trying to gain his trust, you know?"

"He can wait." Rocco pointed to the study. "I'll be brief."

*Why are all the men in my life so bossy?*

"Fine." I hurried into the study, Rocco right behind me. "What's up?"

"I don't think you're prepared for what you're getting into." He joined me on the sofa. "At all."

"Now you sound like your mother." I rolled my eyes because I couldn't keep up with any of them. They told me to marry Romero, and I said I would, but no one thought I could do what they needed. "You don't trust me with this assignment either?"

"I didn't say that."

"What are you saying?"

"I'm saying I wouldn't have put you in this position." He ran his hand through his thick black hair. "I don't question my father, but what he's asking you to do is risky."

"Because you don't think I can do it?"

"I don't know if you can do it, Lu. Not because I don't have faith in you, but because Bilotti is a ruthless son of a bitch. He's a wild card with a mean streak. He's impulsive with his trigger finger."

"But that's not stopping you from sending me in there." I crossed my legs. "Did any of you ever think if this stupid plan doesn't work, Romero will use that trigger finger on me?"

Rocco didn't say anything.

"Of course you didn't, or if you did, none of you care. I'm expendable. I get that."

"That's not true."

"Would you have Sandro to do something this dangerous? Would you send him into enemy territory and ask him to spy to get information?"

"Alessandro can't do this particular job."

"No, only I can." I got up and paced the room. "Now that your dad has put me in this position and given me to Romero in every sense of the word, let me do the job. You'll have to trust me."

"Regardless of what you think, I've always cared about you." He came up from behind me and placed his hand on my shoulder. "When you came to live with us. I'd never had a sister before. I didn't think I needed one, but I did, Lu. I regret a lot of things that this family has done to you through the years. Maybe we weren't the best option when your parents died, but we're your family."

I turned to face him, a lone tear streaming down my cheek. "I don't blame you for the way I've been treated around here. I've always known my place. I may not have liked that place, but I've managed to get through it."

"You've grown into an amazing woman, and I don't want Bilotti to break you." He closed his eyes. "I'll kill him before I let that happen."

"He won't break me." I patted his firm chest. "I'm stronger than you think."

"I know I said I can't second guess my father on this but if this becomes too much, or the minute you think Romero is onto you, I'll get you out."

"Thank you." I kissed his cheek. "That means a lot to me. It'll help to know I have a backup plan."

"No one wants to see you in any danger."

I didn't think that was entirely true. His mother didn't care if I made it out alive.

"I have to go." I scrambled for the door after checking my watch. "I'll be home in time for dinner."

"I want Sam to drive you." He followed me into the foyer.

"Is that necessary?" I was trying to gain Romero's trust. How would he react if I showed up to wherever he was meeting me with a Torrio guard? "I'm driving ten minutes from here."

"It's non-negotiable." He placed his hand on his hip. "Bilotti isn't stupid enough to hurt you. Not now, anyway. But he has enemies, and so does my father. Now that your engagement is public, we have to be extra cautious."

"I understand." I liked it better when I was the throw

away cousin of the clan. No one paid attention to me. I was the last person an enemy would try to use as leverage.

That all changed when Romero put that diamond ring on my finger.

"Be careful." He took out his phone. "I'll text Sam and tell him to bring the car around for you."

"Thank you." I opened the front door. "For the talk too."

I waited by the front gate for Sam to arrive. With each second that passed, I grew more anxious. I had set out with plenty of time to not be late. If I wasn't nervous enough to meet Romero, the thought of being late made me sick to my stomach. He said there would be consequences. What kind of consequences?

"Hey, Sam," I said as he pulled up and opened the door for me. "I'm running a little late."

"Where are we headed?"

"I'll text you the address and you can pop it in the GPS."

"Sure." He got in the front and drove down the long driveway. When he got to the bottom, he stopped and checked his phone. "Dunlap estates. That's a pretty exclusive community. There are only a handful of houses out there."

"Romero asked me to meet him at the address I gave you." I glanced at my watch. "I don't want to be late."

"Okay." He pulled out onto the main road. "I haven't congratulated you."

"That's okay." I didn't feel right lying to Sam, but soon I'd be lying to everyone, even my husband, so did it really matter? "This all happened so fast."

"I never pegged you for the spontaneous type."

"What do you mean?"

"Well, I've been your guard for a few years now, and I've

never seen you meet up with Romero. It surprised me when I heard you were going to marry him."

*You couldn't have been more surprised than me.*

"Not that it's any of my business," he added.

When he focused on the road, I decided it was best to end the conversation. The less I said about it, the better off I would be. It was going to be tough enough keeping up the charade with Romero. I didn't want to create complications. *Who am I kidding?* My whole life was about to become one big complication.

When the car slowed to a stop, I peered out the window. The lights of a police car blared up ahead.

"What's wrong?" I asked. "Why aren't we moving?"

"It looks like there is a down tree in the road from that storm yesterday." He checked his phone. "I'll turn around and see where the GPS reroutes us."

"Will that take much longer?" It was almost five til one and I was definitely going to be late. "I'm supposed to be there at one."

"I'll do my best to get you there as soon as possible, but there aren't many alternative roads into that community. Don't worry, I'm sure your future husband knows you're worth the wait."

"Right." An anxious giggle escaped my lips.

Why hadn't Romero and I thought of exchanging phone numbers? We were so busy fighting with one another the other night, it never even crossed my mind. If it had, I could text him and tell him I was running late.

I rested my head on the back of the seat, closed my eyes, and took a few calming breaths. I had no control over this situation. It wasn't my fault the storm had knocked down a tree and blocked the road. I couldn't help it that Romero picked a meeting point that wasn't easily accessible. He should have thought to give me his number instead of communicating through suspicious packages with creepy gifts.

A few minutes later, Sam found an alternate route. According to the GPS on my phone, it only put us ten minutes out of the way. I wouldn't be that late. Would it matter to Romero?

When we got to the house, Sam drove up and dropped me off at the door. It was a gorgeous two story colonial nestled on a wooded lot. It was massive compared to the other houses in the neighborhood but there was something homey about the property. It didn't at all remind me of the fortress I'd just left.

"I won't be far," he said. "Text me when you're ready to leave."

"Thanks."

I walked up the stone path, taking in the beautifully landscaped grounds. The house was elaborate, but not like the one I grew up in. This was understated compared to that. I liked it.

When I stepped onto the large wraparound porch, Romero was waiting, leaning against the front door. He didn't say anything. He didn't have to. I could already tell by his hard jawline and tense stance that he was pissed off. His dark, brooding mood was sexier than it should have been.

*Too bad I'm the intended target.*

**CHAPTER 10**

*Romero*

Luciana stumbled out of her guard's car and hurried up the pathway. I'd have to replace him once we married. No way would I let a Torrio guard protect what was mine.

She tugged on the hem of her dress as she navigated her way to the porch in ridiculously high heels. They were red. Did she wear them because she knew I liked red? I'd be the first to admit she looked hot. I only wished she could fucking be on time. When she joined me on the porch, I inspected her. She swiped her hair to the side and then fidgeted with the ends. Always so anxious.

"I know I'm late." She beat me to stating the obvious. "There was a road closure, and we had to find an alternate route."

I glanced at my watch.

"I should have left earlier."

"Is there an apology in there somewhere?" My patience was wearing thin with this one.

"I'm sorry." When she straightened her posture, those heels almost put her at eye level with me. "I know being late upsets you."

"More than you can imagine. It tells me you don't respect my time. Like you had more important things to do and keeping me waiting didn't seem to bother you."

"That's not what happened." She shuffled her feet before leaning against the porch railing.

"It won't happen once we're married. Your new security team will make sure of it."

"New security team?" She shook her head. "This wasn't Sam's fault. He didn't know the road would be closed. I don't want a new guard."

"You don't have a choice."

"Why do I need to change my security person?"

"Sam works for your uncle, not for me. I can't have a Torrio guard responsible for you."

"I'm used to Sam." Her lips formed into a sexy pout.

"You'll get used to your new security team." I hadn't decided which one of my men I'd put with her, but whoever it was, I was certain she wouldn't approve.

"I have to get used to a new guard, a new husband, not being able to work for the firm, and whatever else you all decide to throw at me?"

"Pretty much." I shrugged. "I told you the other night to think long and hard about marrying me. There are going to be many changes in your life. Most of them can't be helped."

"What if I can't adapt to these changes?"

"You should walk away right now. While you still can."

I had no intention of letting her leave. I wouldn't allow her to humiliate me now that our engagement had been officially announced. How would it look if a man as powerful as me couldn't keep his woman in line? Her uncle and aunt would probably disown her. Maybe that was what she wanted. It wouldn't be the worst thing in the world for her. If she'd give me a chance, she would see I was the better option.

"I'm not running away." She tried to convince me with those pretty eyes of hers.

"Because you don't have a choice?"

"Do you want me to lie and say something different?"

"I'd like you to give this a chance."

"I'm here, aren't I?"

"Is that what you're calling it? Because I wouldn't call you being present."

She didn't answer me and that frustrated the hell out of me. I'd never wanted to know what someone was thinking more than I wanted to know what was going on in that pretty little head of hers. I was good at reading people, but with her I didn't understand what was going on.

"It is a less than ideal situation for you, but can you honestly say your life was all that spectacular before you agreed to marry me?"

"What do you know about my life?"

"I know that your family didn't give it a second thought when they promised you to me. Your uncle and your cousins don't even like me, butterfly. What does that say about how they feel about you? How they value you?"

"You're wrong."

"Am I? Why would they hand you over to me so freely?"

"They have their reasons." She looked down at her feet. "I mean, doesn't this benefit both families?"

"What do you know about their reasons?" I studied her expression but as usual, she didn't give me much.

"Nothing," she answered too fast for my liking. "No one tells me anything. You're right, they promised me to you without a second thought. It's crystal clear what they think of me."

Obviously, this was a touchy subject. The more I thought about it, the more I thought the Torrios weren't doing this for all the reasons they had stated. I'd have to investigate a little more before I made a move. If they thought about betraying me, there would be hell to pay, and I didn't care who was caught in the crossfire.

"Are you ready to see our new house?" I asked.

"What?" She gazed at the house behind me. "This is our house?"

"I bought it for us to start our life together."

"Oh."

*Oh? That was all she could manage?*

I pushed open the door and led her into the foyer. She bit her bottom lip as she looked around at the high ceilings and the grand staircase that led to the landing that overlooked most of the downstairs. That was my favorite feature. I liked being able to see the lower level from upstairs. No surprises.

The property was set back in the woods in a gated community. It would be tough for anyone to get in here without my team knowing. I had already started moving operations from the penthouse to this location. I wanted to be up and running by the time we were married.

She didn't move from the foyer. It was hard to tell what she thought. Her big, uncertain eyes gave little away.

"It's bright and airy." She moved toward the stairs. "It's very pretty."

"Does that mean you like it?"

She nodded.

What would it take to impress her? "I know it's not the mansion you're used to living in but it's not a shack either."

"I didn't say it was."

"You didn't say much of anything."

She was just as bad as her snobby family. I thought since she wasn't a true Torrio she would be less judgmental. It didn't appear that way. I'd spent a fortune on this place, having to buy out the original purchaser to get such an impressive property. Why did it bother me so much that she wasn't jumping up and down with excitement or showing me the least bit of her approval?

*Fuck that!* I didn't get this far to have some second-rate mafia princess make me feel less of a man. I needed to show her exactly what she was getting into.

"Upstairs." I pointed to the staircase.

"What?" She backed away from me, but I advanced her. "Why?"

"Maybe the bedroom will impress you."

"We don't have to…" She stepped back, hitting the banister and losing her footing. I caught her by the elbow. "I'm sure it's fine"

"Let's go." I took her by the hand and guided her up the stairs, but she kept stumbling in those heels. "I expect it will be better than fine."

Once we got to the top of the stairs, she stopped walking. When I turned and glared at her, she let go of my hand.

"What's the problem?" I wasn't sure I had the patience for this woman. No one had ever turned down an invitation to go into a bedroom with me before.

"It's just that I've never…" She motioned toward the bedroom. "You know."

"Are you trying to tell me you're a virgin?"

"Yes."

An enormous amount of relief came over me. I didn't know why it mattered so much, but if I was going to marry for territory and connections, I should at least get the honor of popping my wife's cherry.

"I'm pleased with that revelation." I took her hand and continued down the hall. "Your uncle and your cousins suspected but they couldn't guarantee it."

"Sandro could."

"Really?" Why didn't the youngest Torrio speak up when I had asked?

"I tell him everything. Well, not in detail, but he knows I've never been with anyone."

"You should be happy to know he kept your confidence when I asked."

"Why would you ask?"

We stopped when we reached the double doors of the master suite.

"Because it's my right to know."

"It seems like such an uncouth thing to ask my uncle and his sons." She shot me a disgusted look, and I despised the way it made me feel. "You could have asked me."

"I planned on asking you today." I pushed open the bedroom doors. "Among other things."

"What things?"

"We're going to play a little game of truth or dare, but I'll make up the rules as we go and you'll abide."

"I don't understand."

"You will."

Once inside the bedroom, she took a moment to look around, moving toward the window and creating some distance between us. I slipped off my suit jacket and draped it over the chair in the sitting room. This was the only room

I'd had furnished so far. I wanted to make sure the bed was here on our wedding night.

When I came up behind her, she tensed. I didn't know whether to commend her on her keen instincts or be annoyed that she shied away from me. She had so many bad habits I'd have to break her from.

"What do you think of our bedroom?" I removed her black leather jacket and tossed it on the chair a few feet away.

"I didn't realize we'd be sharing a bedroom."

"That's what married people do." I moved her hair to one side and ran my lips along her neck. "Share things."

"We don't even know each other. Can't I sleep in another room for a few weeks?"

"That won't work for me."

When I lowered the zipper on her dress, she spun around. "No."

"No, we won't be sharing a bedroom?" I gripped her forearms and yanked her toward me. "Or, no, don't take off your dress?"

"Don't take off my dress."

"Then how are we going to play my game?" I lowered my lips to her throat as I trailed my fingers to the back of her dress. "I want this off."

"Why?"

"You'll see."

She closed her eyes, but didn't protest when I eased the zipper and pushed the dress from her shoulders, letting it fall to her feet.

"Step out of it. But leave the heels on."

I held her hand, helping her move away from the crumpled white fabric at her feet. Her olive-colored skin was a stark contrast to her pale pink bra and panties. My cock hardened when I spied her pert nipples straining against the lace.

She fiddled with her hands as she rocked back and forth. Her anxiety unsettled me because it was something I didn't experience personally. I did what I wanted and dealt with the fallout after. The people I associated with had nerves of steel. I surrounded myself with strong, unforgiving people.

"You don't have to be shy around me." I circled my thumb around her nipple. "You're perfect."

She put her head down, but I wanted her to look at me, so I took her chin between my fingers and tilted her face to meet my gaze.

"You don't believe me," I said.

Why couldn't she take the compliment?

"No one has ever told me I'm perfect."

"That must mean you surround yourself with small-minded people."

She didn't really surround herself with many people. According to the file my guy had on her, she didn't have any friends other than her cousins. She stayed home almost all the time other than going to work.

"I'd like to see more of you." I popped the clasp on the front of her bra, freeing her breasts. *Amazing.* Suddenly, I didn't feel like marrying her was going to be such a burden. A virgin who I could mold into anything I wanted. Not a terrible deal at all.

She tried to cross her arms in front of her chest, but I held them at her sides.

"Don't deny me." I pressed my lips to the corner of her mouth. "I'm going to ask you a few questions and I want the absolute truth."

Her breath hitched in her throat when I gripped her hips and pulled her close to me.

"We'll start with something easy." I ogled her lips, trying hard to resist the urge to claim them. "Has anyone kissed you on the mouth before?"

"Yes," she whispered.

I expected that to be her answer. If she'd said no, I would have known she was lying. No twenty-two-year-old could be that innocent. Although, I'd bet this one had little experience.

"How many?"

"A few." Her voice was low, and she seemed almost ashamed of her answer.

I took her hands in mine, stepping back so I could admire her almost naked body. "Has anyone's fingers been inside you?"

"One time."

That was disappointing, but I couldn't expect her to be totally inexperienced.

I ran my finger along the edge of her panties. "Did he make you come, my filthy girl?"

"No."

"Has any man ever made you come?"

She shook her head.

"Are you wet for me?"

She didn't answer, but her skin flushed an alluring shade of pink. My cock liked this shy, virginal, babe-in-woods routine.

"I can see for myself." I slid my hand inside her panties and rubbed my finger along her slick entrance. At first, she squirmed against my touch, but after a few seconds she relaxed.

She pressed her palm against my shoulder when I

inserted my fingers inside her, moving them in and out in a slow rhythm.

"I can make you come." I removed my hand from inside her panties. "Remember when I said there would be consequences if you were late?"

"Yes."

"You're about to find out exactly what I meant by that."

**CHAPTER 11**

*Luciana*

Staring into Romero's emerald eyes, answering his questions while I was practically naked was a little unsettling, but I didn't hate it.

What did he plan to do with me today? A nervous energy engulfed me, but there was also an odd anticipation. I didn't want him to take things all the way, but I wanted more.

"You shouldn't have been late." He gripped my chin between his fingers, squeezing firmly enough to leave fingerprints on my skin. "Let's talk about this mouth of yours. How many cocks have passed these luscious lips?"

I spoke a little louder this time because I wanted him to know he could be the first. "None."

"I can't wait to remedy that."

When he released my chin, I looked down, catching the view of his prominent erection straining against his pants.

"See something you like?"

I glanced away, embarrassed that he'd caught me ogling at him through his pants.

"At first, I thought this innocent routine was an act. Something you thought I might like." He traced his fingertips over my nipples one at a time. "I like it a lot. It makes me what to fuck you so hard, but it isn't an act, is it? You are as pure as you appear."

"I don't get out much."

"That's not going to change when you marry me." He kissed the top of my shoulder as he played with the ends of my hair. "I might keep you locked up here and keep you all to myself."

He brushed his lips along my collarbone. His warm breath set my body ablaze.

"I like the idea of you being here all the time whenever I want to fuck you," he said.

I squeezed my legs together, trying to create some friction. The idea of him wanting me intrigued me. It shouldn't have. I was being sold to him, no matter what my family said about being a spy. They were still marrying me off to a man they knew I'd have to lie beside every night and give him whatever he asked of me.

"You like that thought, don't you, butterfly?"

"Why do you keep calling me that?"

"Because you're delicate and vulnerable." He trailed his lips to mine, swiping them along my mouth. Not a kiss but he was so close. It was intimate and strange. "It's my job to protect you now. To keep you safe."

"I don't need your protection." Unless he could protect me from him, I didn't see any other threats.

"We'll see."

He took my hand and led me over to the cream-colored leather sofa in the sitting area of the master suite. The warm gray tones accentuated the spectacular room. The pristine hardwood floors appeared to have never been walked on before. Everything smelled clean and new, but there was a prominent scent that seemed familiar. I remembered it from our engagement party. When he was close, I picked up the aroma of a deep, spicy scent. Like cinnamon and ginger. It made me want to cuddle him on a cold winter night. Only, he didn't seem like the cuddling type.

He locked me in his gaze as he removed his tie. A devious smirk crossed his lips before he spun me around and pressed his chest against my back. He took my wrists in his hands and then captured them between the silk of his tie. He bound my hands together, securing them in a tight knot.

"What are you doing?" I looked over my shoulder, panic rising in my voice at the thought of giving up control to him.

"Punishing you."

"What, no!" I lunged forward a bit too fast and my stupid heels made me stumble and trip. Romero caught me by the waist, holding me against him.

"Settle down." He kissed the side of my neck. "We don't want bruises on that pretty face for our wedding day. What would people think?"

"I don't like this game." Being restrained frightened me, especially since he was the one doing it. He was already scary enough without retraining me up. "I don't want to be punished. I don't want to be tied up. I don't like this game."

"Give it a chance. How do you know you don't like it if you don't try?" He snaked his hands up my stomach, cupping my breasts and squeezing hard. "Do you want to feel how punishing you affects me?"

"I... I don't know."

"Get on your knees." He growled against my ear. "I'll show you."

I tensed when he undid his belt buckle and lowered his

zipper. I couldn't see what he was doing, but it wasn't difficult to figure out.

"Why haven't you done what I told you to do?" He shoved me down on my knees, causing my chest to fall forward onto the cool leather couch. "That's better."

He dropped to his knees behind me, pulling me up so my back was flush with his solid, muscular chest.

"Please." I glanced over my shoulder. "I don't want to. Not like this."

"You don't want to what?" He gathered my hair in his hand and tugged my head back. "Fuck?"

I closed my eyes and tried to control my breathing as he pushed me forward onto the couch, pressing on my back so that I arched my hips. He gripped my thighs and spread my legs apart. I struggled under his rough hold, but he didn't give me much room to move.

"Don't worry." He slipped his finger under the elastic of my panties and pushed inside me. "I'm not giving you my cock today, but I know you want it. You wouldn't be this wet if you didn't."

When he inched closer to me, the heat of his body transferred onto me. He increased his pace with his fingers inside me, making me forget how nervous I'd been. An odd sensation of pleasure took over. I rocked my hips in rhythm with his fingers, trying to get him to make me feel good.

Confusion cluttered my brain. Why did this feel so fantastic? I didn't even like Romero, but yet, my body responded to him.

He withdrew his fingers and pressed his tip at my entrance, before rubbing it along my clit. My muscles clenched, and I tried to scoot away, but he wrapped his arm around my waist and held me still.

"I told you I wouldn't today." He shifted his hips forward,

sliding his length between my legs, and massaged it against me.

With each thrust of his hips, his breathing became heavier. The only barrier between us was the silk of my panties, making it easy to feel his thick, swollen shaft as he ran it back and forth.

My nipples kneaded against the cold leather of the couch, stimulating me further. He took my hips in his firm hold, moving my compliant frame in time with his as he dry humped me into oblivion.

"Do you like this?" He dug his fingers into my hips. "Wait until I give it to you for real."

My legs shook beneath me as he continued to bring us both to release. I'd soaked through my panties. My body trembled with raw need as the building inside my core shot lower, spasming between my legs. I teetered on the edge of insanity, but before I benefited from the endgame, Romero grunted. I jerked forward when a hot stream of liquid coated my back.

"My cum looks good on you, Luciana." He slapped my backside hard enough for it to sting before getting up and walking away.

I stayed in the position he'd put me in with my hands still restrained behind my back, covered in his ejaculation. I should have been disgusted, but there was something sexy about this situation.

He joined me on the floor and washed my back with a warm, wet towel. He'd even thought to get a dry one to wipe away the wetness the first had caused. His actions weren't rough like they usually were, and that took me by surprise.

He turned me to face him. He lowered his lips to my jaw and ran them down my neck as he reached behind me and freed my hands.

I draped my arms over his shoulders and brought my mouth close to his. We hadn't kissed yet, but I needed to feel his lips against mine. My body hummed with desire.

He didn't indulge me. Instead, he stood, and strode over to the chair and put his suit jacket back on.

"Next time, be on time and maybe, I'll let you come too."

"You disgusting pig!" If I had something to throw at him, I would have, but he was gone before I could process what had happened.

He left me on the floor of our new bedroom, alone, humiliated, and aroused. So very aroused. I sat back and rested my head on the couch, spreading my legs and slipping my hand between them. As I closed my eyes, I thought about him touching me, making me beg for more. Within seconds, I exploded my release, biting my lip so I didn't scream.

*I hate you, Romero Bilotti...*

*How could I marry such an insensitive monster? In a few days, I'd have the answer to that question unless I found a way to escape.*

**CHAPTER 12**

*Romero*

I hadn't spoken to Luciana since I'd shown her the bedroom. She'd stormed down the steps and ran out of here so fast, I figured it was best to let her cool down. Her family promised to keep her under lock and key until today... our wedding day.

I took the little black box out of my desk drawer and popped it open. The sparkly wedding band was next to the platinum one that I had purchased for myself. In a few hours, my mother's wedding band would belong to Luciana. I'd never thought about who I would give it to. I didn't consider myself the marrying type, but now that I was getting hitched, I didn't mind putting the ring on Luciana's finger.

Sure, she despised me, but most women did, which was why I didn't consider myself husband material. Circumstances change. Opportunities present themselves. My new wife would have to get used to me. What choice did she have? I could give her a good life.

When Gio barged into my study, I shoved the rings back into my desk drawer.

"Why are you working?" he asked.

"Why can't you knock?"

"Someone has wedding jitters."

"Fuck off."

My brother was already dressed in his tux. He carried in a black garment bag and hung it on the back of the door.

"Dude, you're getting married soon. Shouldn't you be getting ready?"

"All I have to do is shower and put on my tux." I put my feet up on my desk. "When you're this good looking, it doesn't take much."

"God, help us."

"What's the status on Arturo?"

"Are you sure you want to discuss business today? We can take a day off, you know."

"Today is business for me. When I say *I do*, we gain more than we ever thought possible when we started out." Luciana was a bonus. "What's the situation with Arturo?"

"It doesn't look good." Gio sat down in the chair across from my desk. "He hasn't resurfaced, and neither has our money."

I pounded my fist on my desk. "I want him found!"

"I'm doing the best I can, but you have to face the possibility that if someone doesn't want him to be found, he won't be found. Think about what you would do if you were hiding a body."

"There would be no reason to kill Arturo and not send a message." I leaned back in my chair. "If he stole from us, we have to find him and deal with him. If his disappearance is retaliation, we have to find out why and who is behind it. Why take out one of our top people and not take responsibility for it? What would someone gain by doing that?"

"It makes little sense."

There was a knock at the open door. When I looked up, it was my head security guy, Joey, standing there. Most of the guys were getting ready to attend the wedding, but he wanted to stay behind and look after me.

"What?" I asked.

"You have company," he said. "The Torrio brothers."

"Interesting." I nodded at Gio. "Can't wait to see what they have to say."

"Why would they show up here?" Gio stood and straightened his jacket. "They're going to see us later."

"Should I let them in?" Joey asked.

"Yeah, why not?" What could they want today? "Is everything in place for my bride's security?"

"Yes, Jag is already at the Torrio estate."

"Good." I pointed toward the hall. "Show my guests in."

"Jag?" Gio asked.

"I thought he'd be the best option for Luciana. She's already upset that she has to give up her guard, but I can't have a Torrio employee looking after my wife. Jag has been with us for a while and I can trust he won't try anything with her."

"So, you vetted her security based on whether you could trust they won't try to fuck her?" Gio shook his head. "Don't they all know you would kill them if they tried anything?"

"They should, but why irritate myself? Jag is a good fit, and he deserved the promotion." Not only would I be trusting him with my wife, but he could keep an eye on her and report back to me anything I needed to know. It was a sensitive position. He had to gain her trust but stay loyal to me.

Vincent, Rocco, and Alessandro walked into my study, already dressed for the wedding. I stood from my chair and invited them in.

"Thank you for seeing us." Vincent shook my hand. "We won't take up much of your time."

"I didn't expect to see you before the ceremony." I glanced at my watch. "Is this a business call? If it is, your timing is impeccable."

"Why is that?" Vincent asked.

"We were discussing the disappearance of one of my lieutenants." I studied each of their faces, but none of them gave anything away. "He's been missing for longer than I would like."

"I'm sorry to hear that," Vincent said. "We could look around for you. See if we find anything suspicious."

"I'd appreciate that."

"We're practically family," he said.

"In a few hours, we will be family," I reminded him. "How is my beautiful bride?"

"Pissed." Alessandro glared at me. "Whatever you did to her the last time you were together really made her mad."

"Well, that's unfortunate." It pleased me to know that my punishment was so effective. If she was still mad about it, she got my message. I'd been thinking about her perky tits and adorable ass all week.

"She's not happy with you," Sandro said.

"We had a misunderstanding." I went to the bar in the corner of the room and took out my best bottle of vodka. "I'm sure she'll get over it." I pointed to the bottle. "This is a wedding gift from one of my Russian associates."

My little butterfly was still upset with me. That should make for an interesting wedding ceremony.

"I wouldn't count on it," Sandro said. "She can hold a grudge."

"Must be her Sicilian blood." Rocco laughed. "It's going to be a cold wedding night for you."

*Somehow, I doubt that.* "I'm sure I can smooth things over with her."

"We didn't come to talk about your wedding night," Vincent said.

"I can't wait to hear what you have to say." After I poured the vodka, Gio handed out the glasses to everyone. "We can have a drink to celebrate my nuptials and you can tell me what I can do for you."

"We know this situation between you and Lu isn't normal. Most people don't marry off a family member to a complete stranger," Vincent said.

"Unless that family gains substantially by doing so." I sipped my drink. "As all of you are."

"We're not the only ones gaining," Rocco said. "This arrangement benefits all of us."

"Hey, I know what I'm getting, but your family approached me. I didn't proposition anyone, and I didn't suggest that I marry your little cousin. Your parents did that."

I didn't want to bad-mouth their mother because I wouldn't want anyone disrespecting mine, but if they had heard the things that woman said about Luciana, I didn't think any of them would agree with the situation.

"We have to make sure you understand who she is," Rocco said. "Lu is a shy girl. She keeps to herself. She can be awkward. Our cousin has lived a sheltered life and sometimes that shows."

"She likes to read and binge watch old TV shows,"

Sandro said. "She enjoys going to the movie theater, and she loves butter on her popcorn."

"She can still do all of that." I shrugged. "I won't stop her."

"I thought maybe you'd want to know some things about her. It will help you get to know her better. She's afraid to come live here." He swirled the vodka around in his glass. "She's not used to being in strange places."

"She went away to school." I remembered Antonio telling me she lived away for four years.

"High school," Sandro said. "She hated it. No one wanted to be her friend because she was a Torrio. She begged our father to let her come home, but he thought it was better if she stayed there."

Hell, the more they talked, the more sympathetic I became, and it was rare for me to feel bad for anyone.

"My father sent her to that school because he wanted to keep her away from our world." Vincent clenched his jaw. "He was trying to do something good, but it wasn't best for Lu. She stuck it out but I know it was a nightmare for her. We're hoping this arrangement isn't going to be horrible for her."

"How much does she know about your business?" I asked.

"We don't tell her much and she doesn't ask questions," Vincent said. "Sometimes, we think she's a little odd, but she has a big heart. If you break it, we're going to have a problem."

This conversation would be laughable, considering they were all going to watch me marry their cousin, knowing it wasn't what she wanted. I had learned so much about Luciana in the last few minutes.

I wouldn't insult them by dismissing their concerns. She

didn't seem to have much in this world. She had money and lived in a big house, but I could see the loneliness in her eyes. She was a beautiful woman, but her spark was missing. Maybe these three men standing in front of me were the only people who kept her going all these years. If that were true, I could feel some gratitude toward them.

"Don't hurt her," Rocco said. "I'll make you die painfully if you do."

"Don't threaten my brother." Gio placed his glass on my desk.

"It's okay, Gio." I held up my hand. "I can appreciate where they are coming from even if I don't understand how they could consider a family member so expendable."

"She's not expendable," Sandro said.

"I know you believe that, Alessandro." I looked at Vincent and Rocco. "Can the two of you say the same?"

"We deal in a brutal world." Vincent finished his drink. "We have to do things we're not always proud of, but we do them because we don't have a choice. Our families have come to an agreement. All we're asking is that you treat our cousin well. She's been through so much in her short life."

"I'll treat her exactly as she deserves."

I didn't know Luciana well enough yet, but I knew her loyalties were with her family. I didn't blame her for that, but when she said her vows, she was going to have to prove to me I was the one she would stand beside when push came to shove.

"Now, if you'll excuse me, I have a wedding to get ready for." I shook each of their hands. "Gio will show you out. I'll see you later."

They said their goodbyes, each of them judging me as if I was some lowlife who was trying to steal their innocent cousin under the cover of darkness. These self-righteous assholes were in the same business I was. They were no better than me. If anything, they were far worse. They were giving her to a ruthless arms dealer with no conscience. At least I knew who I was. Did they?

If they only knew what I was really capable of. Would they have still promised her hand?

It was time for me to find out who I was dealing with. I'd done some surface background checks on the entire Torrio clan when Giancarlo approached me with their initial offer. Now it was time to figure out who they really were.

Gio came back into the study. "They're gone. I don't trust them."

"I'm already on it." I took out my phone and searched my contacts for my investigator. "I'll get everything I need on them."

"Shouldn't we have done that before we agreed to this alliance?"

"Before we didn't have the leverage we have today."

That brief visit from the brothers' Torrio was more enlightening to me than the three of them could ever have imagined.

"What leverage?" Gio asked.

"My new bride." I smirked because not only was I marrying a stunning woman who would warm my bed every night, but I might have found a weak spot among the Torrios. One I hadn't seen before. "As long as I have her, nothing is going to stop us."

## CHAPTER 13

*Luciana*

This was happening and I couldn't stop the nightmare.

I stood in front of my closet, staring at the gorgeous white silk designer gown hanging on display. It was delivered last night. All the alterations had been made and it fit me to perfection. My hair and makeup were professionally done an hour ago. I had the shoes, the enormous engagement ring, and the obnoxious groom. What a fairytale! I could already see tomorrow's headlines:

*Mafia princess marries heartless kingpin in the arranged marriage of the decade.*

Well, at least that was what it would say if I wrote it. I'm sure my uncle's people already fed the media exactly what they wanted the spin to be. If it were anything like the engagement party press the day after that fiasco, everyone would believe that this union was built on love and free-will. Why shouldn't they believe that? Wasn't that why most people got married? Except in this scenario, I wasn't most people. I was an unwilling pawn in a deadly game.

*I don't want to do this. I can't do this.*

I picked up the frame on my dresser and stared at my parents. They were young and vibrant, and so in love. What would my life have been like if they weren't taken from me all those years ago in that horrible car accident? I would have had choices and freedom. My wedding day would have looked drastically different, too. I'd be marrying a good, kind-hearted man. One who loved me. There would be no deals or alliances. No violence or bloodshed. I wouldn't have to pretend that all of this was okay with me.

*Fuck my life!*

I paced the bedroom, gazing out the window. Was I actually considering climbing out of a window to escape? Stupid idea. It would never work. Even if I didn't break my ankle trying to run, I wouldn't get past the guards. If by some miracle I did, where would I go? If my family didn't find me, which they would, my soon-to-be husband would track me down. Not because he loved me and couldn't live without me. No, this was much more complicated than that. He had to marry me to get what he wanted from my family. I had to marry him to get intel on him.

*Deep breaths, Lu.*

You can do this. People didn't always stay married forever. This wasn't a death sentence. Focus on your goals. Law school. All I had to do was get through this crazy part of my life and I'd get out of here. They would have to let me go.

If they didn't trust Romero and it was a double cross, they would cut ties with him or... well, take him out. If there was nothing incriminating against him, the two families could work together and they wouldn't need me. Why would they? The alliance would be in place and they could all trust one another, and I could go away. Far away and start over again. Not as a Torrio and definitely not as a Bilotti.

*Luciana Bilotti.*

Who would she even be? A desperate mafia wife who obeyed her vicious husband's every command? No identity of her own? *No way!* It didn't matter what vows I took today. I would never be his wife. Not in the real sense. I was in survival mode now.

The swift knock caused me to fumble with the frame, but instead of crashing to the floor, it landed on the bed. When I opened the door, I found my uncle standing on the other side. He was dressed for the wedding in his perfectly tailored tuxedo. Everyone would play a part today.

"Can I come in?" He didn't wait for me to answer as he stepped inside. *Typical.* "I see you're almost ready for your big day."

"As ready as I can be."

He picked up the picture of my parents and studied it, but he didn't say anything. He placed the frame on the dresser.

"The house has been completely transformed," he said. "The grounds are perfect for a spectacular wedding venue. Your aunt has outdone herself."

"I'm sure it's fabulous." How couldn't it be? My aunt had spared no expense for this show.

"You look distressed." He stepped toward me. "Are you okay?"

*Is he serious?*

"I'm holding it together as best as I can." I smiled. "Aren't all brides supposed to be nervous?"

"I suppose." He reached into his inside tuxedo pocket and took out a silver chain with a cross embedded with diamonds.

"What is that?"

"It belonged to your mother." He glanced down at the necklace and then back at me.

Were his eyes softer than usual?

"Oh." I studied the delicate piece of jewelry displayed in his hand. "It's beautiful."

"Our grandmother gave it to her. My sister cherished it."

"I think I remember it. Seeing it now reminds me of her."

I didn't have a ton of memories of my parents. I was ten when I came to live here and it was as if they were completely forgotten. No one talked about them. I used to ask questions, but my aunt and uncle never really answered them. After a while, I stopped asking. I wasn't given any closure and although it had been years since their deaths, I still grieved them. I longed to know them.

"She had it on the night she..." He cleared his throat. "I kept it for you. I wanted to give it to you for a special occasion and although you may not agree that today is a special day, it is."

"My wedding day." Was he here to make me believe that marrying Romero was a good thing for me? Like any of this was my idea? He did realize that in a world where I had a choice, Romero wouldn't be my first or even my seventh choice. "I'm going through with it but you're right, I don't consider it special."

"That's not why it's special."

"What do you mean?"

"I know you don't want to marry Romero, and I can't say that I blame you. It was a huge ask on my part and I wouldn't have asked if I didn't think I could trust you."

"I appreciate your trust."

"I have complete faith that you will get the information this family needs to take down the Bilotti empire."

"Take him down?" When had that been part of the arrangement? I would admit I knew little, and I was afraid to ask questions, but I didn't agree to taking away his business. "I thought you wanted me to find out if you could trust him?"

"That's a big part of your assignment but I know I can't trust him."

"Then why are we going through with this?"

"I need you to help retake what is rightfully mine."

"Rightfully yours? I thought you took over the Bilotti territory after Romero's father was murdered."

"You've been researching?" He chuckled. "I should have figured you would. Your nose is always in a book or on the internet. You know more about the firm's cases than my sons do."

"Isn't anything Romero built these last fifteen years his? His territory has nothing to do with what his father built."

"I respect you educating yourself on the dynamics of all of this, but you don't need to concern yourself with any of that. All you have to do is bring me information on what he's doing and who he's doing it with. I'll handle the rest."

"I didn't think, I mean, this isn't what I agreed to."

"You'll agree to whatever I tell you to agree to. The plan has changed and now you'll change with it."

"What if he's too secretive and I can't get those details?"

"You'll have to get creative."

"He doesn't seem like a stupid man. I don't even think he likes me that much."

"Nonsense. What's not to like?"

I could think of a few things. Number one being, I was about to betray him in the worst possible way. He was going into this marriage because he thought he was creating an alliance that would make both families stronger. There was tension between Romero and my family, but Romero was a lucrative businessman. He wouldn't have done this if he didn't think he would gain from it.

"Here." My uncle stood behind me and clasped my mother's cross around my neck. "Now you have a piece of her. I never realized how much you look like her. She was such a beautiful girl. She'll watch over you and protect you."

"How much of her protection am I going to need?" I placed my hand over the small cross, feeling closer to my mom than I had in years.

"There's no need for you to worry about anything." He pulled me into a hug, taking me by surprise. He'd never shown me much affection in all the years I'd been with him. "This family will never forget your sacrifice today."

"I won't let you down."

"Sandro told me about your plans to ask me about law school." He released me from his hold. "You're an ambitious woman."

"I was going to ask you before you asked me to marry Romero. I was still hoping to when the time was right."

"When this job is over and I have what I need from the Bilotti family, I'll honor your request and send you to law school."

"You will?" A genuine smile graced my lips. I hadn't smiled for real in a long time. "Thank you. I know I can do it."

"You're proving yourself today, Lu." He opened the bedroom door. "It would be a major asset to have you as an attorney in my firm."

*That isn't what I had in mind.*

"You better get dressed. You don't want to be late for your own wedding."

Once he left, I sat on the bed and processed what he had said. He had changed the rules of this assignment an hour before I had to marry Romero. Spying on him to see if he was a worthy business associate was much different from collecting information so my uncle could steal his business. I didn't have a choice either way, but I didn't have any desire to ruin Romero. Lying, cheating, spying, and deceiving weren't words I would have associated myself with a few weeks ago, but that was who my family was forcing me to be.

I got up and went over to my wedding dress, running the silk between my fingers. As I reached for the hanger, another knock at the door interrupted me. When had I ever been this popular? At this rate, I'd never be on time.

My visitor knocked again, harder and louder this time. *What the hell?* What could be so important?

"I'm coming." I made my way to the door and pulled it open, ready to yell at Sandro for being so impatient. Only it wasn't Sandro.

A chill ran down my spine, and my stomach flipped with terror. Seeing him threw me into reality.

In an hour, I would be his.

"Hello, Luciana." Romero barged into the room and shut the door behind him. "I hear you're upset with me."

I swallowed back my nerves, trying not to think about the last time we were together. Over the last few days, I'd been furious at him for leaving me alone after he'd taken his pleasure from me. Now that he stood in front of me, I didn't have the guts to tell him off.

"What are you doing here?" I asked.

"Getting married." He smirked. "But first, I have a gift for you."

"Leave." I pointed to the door because I didn't want him here. It was bad enough I'd have to give myself to him in front of a room full of strangers. "You shouldn't be here."

"I'll be anywhere I want to be."

"You're not supposed to see me before the ceremony."

"Please." He laughed. "I don't believe in any of that bullshit. We're going to make our own rules, sweetheart."

When he yanked me toward him, my satin robe draped off my shoulders, revealing my white lace corset. "Nice, is that for me?"

He tugged on the belt of the robe, spreading it open and taking in every inch of me with the lust of a hungry animal.

*Why do I like the attention?*

"White looks good on you, my sweet innocent bride." He licked his lips. "I look forward to corrupting you in ways you've never imagined, my little virgin."

**CHAPTER 14**

*Romero*

What I wouldn't give to take her innocence right now. She looked too fucking hot standing in front of me in her underwear. Her breasts spilled out of the top of the corset and her white panties taunted me.

*We're almost there.* In a few hours, I would be the first man to claim her. The only man who would ever have her.

Over the last few days, I'd thought about what it would mean to be her husband. When I'd agreed to this alliance, I hadn't really thought past what I would gain from it from a business standpoint. Even when I'd put the engagement ring on her finger and Antonio introduced us as a couple, it still didn't kick in for me. She was going to be my wife, but what did that mean?

I could try to make a go of it. We couldn't be husband and wife on paper only. She had to understand that this was a genuine commitment. I had men under me who admired me. Business associates who respected me. Enemies who feared me. I couldn't have a rogue wife. That would be a sign of weakness. Some could try to use my vulnerability against me.

When I married Luciana, all the families in the organization would believe that she was mine in every sense of the word. Making her believe it would prove to be a challenge. But when had I ever backed down from a challenge? Getting her in line might be one of the most exciting things I'd done in a long time. I had a feeling we were both going to enjoy this wild ride. Starting right now...

"Did you miss me?" I asked, holding her close.

"Get out!" She shoved at my chest in a sad attempt to push me out the door. "How did you even get in here? I have security."

She was a little kitten trying to be a lion. *Cute.*

"Right, about that." She wasn't going to like what I had to say next, but did she ever like anything I had to say? "As of this morning, your security team transitioned to my men."

"What?"

"Your lead guard's name is Jag and he will take exceptional care of you." I glanced at the suitcases and boxes stacked in the corner of the room. "I'll have him load those into the car."

"What about Sam?"

"We've already been through this. He works for your uncle, and you're my responsibility now."

"I know, but I thought I'd have a chance to say goodbye to him."

"You're getting married, not moving to Belize. You'll be back here from time to time. You'll see him again." I held her close to me, breathing in her sweet scent. "Your muscles are so tense. You need to chill a bit."

"All these changes are stressing me out. It's too much, too soon."

"You let me take care of you. That's my job now."

"I can't."

I ignored her resistance because whether or not she liked it, I would take care of her. "You look beautiful."

Her hair was piled in loose curls on top of her head, and she had on more makeup than usual. Her eyebrows were darker, and her lashes much longer. I preferred her natural face, but there was something quite alluring about her today.

She glanced down, too shy to accept my compliment. "You should go."

"Why?"

"Because I have to get dressed."

"We have a few minutes and I prefer you naked." I pressed my erection against her thigh. "We have enough time for me to give you your gift."

"No." She twisted out of my hold and stepped back, tripping over the comforter at the end of the bed.

I caught her and scooped her up in my arms.

"As much as I like the chase, we're going to have to save that for later."

"Put me down!" She smacked my shoulder. "What are you doing?"

"Whatever the fuck I want."

When I tossed her onto the bed, she bounced, causing some of the spiral curls to fall over her face.

"We can't get married when you're so upset with me." I crawled between her legs. "I know why you're mad and I also know how to fix it."

"I don't want you to fix anything." She thrashed her legs. "Stop it!"

"Be quiet or I'll put a gag in your mouth." I gripped her thighs. "Don't anger me."

She trembled when I slid her panties down her legs and flung them on the floor. In a few seconds, she wouldn't be afraid. I spread her thighs and moved between them.

"What are you doing?"

"You can't be that innocent." I licked her smooth mound. "Lie back and enjoy."

I scooted her center closer to me, inhaling her unique scent.

"Do you really want to start our new lives together being so hostile toward me?" I pushed my fingers inside her. "The sooner you realize what you're getting yourself into, the better off you'll be."

She squirmed when I lowered my face between her legs.

"Stay still," I ordered. "If you don't relax, I'm the only one who will get any pleasure out of this."

"No, don't."

"Don't what?" I swirled my tongue along her clit. "Do that?"

Spreading her open with my thumb and finger, I inserted my tongue inside her, licking her hot folds.

"How about that? Should I stop doing that?"

"Yes," she said, but her throaty response betrayed her. "We can't do this."

"I can do this all night, baby."

With a sweet moan, she raised her hips off the bed, rocking her pussy into my face.

For a girl who was so against a tongue fuck, she sure wasn't complaining now. I lifted her leg and draped it over my shoulder. My balls ached when I pushed my fingers deep inside her. She was tighter than I expected and as she clenched around my fingers, all I could think about was burying my cock in her.

*Soon... so soon.*

If it were up to me, I'd skip the whole charade of the reception and have the minister marry us right in this bedroom. Then I could lock the door and fuck her right after. But then I'd prove to the Torrios I was every bit the savage, unrefined jerk they all thought I was. As much as I despised this family, I would give Luciana a proper wedding day.

"Romero..." she moaned.

I loved the way she said my name when she was on the verge of an orgasm. I could get used to that.

She gripped the comforter and thrust her pelvis in time with my tongue and fingers. *Fuck!* I shoved my hips into the bed, trying to relieve the pressure in my cock. This little virgin was going to make me come into my tuxedo pants if I didn't finish her off soon. Flattening my tongue, I licked her in long, slow strokes until she shook against me.

"Oh..." She ran her fingers through my hair.

She sighed as she dropped her hips back on the mattress and came into my mouth.

I lapped up her juices, licking and kissing her inner thighs. Releasing her from my hold, I rubbed my fingers over the red marks I'd left behind. There would be plenty more where they came from. I longed to mark all of her with my fingers, teeth, and lips.

Her erratic breathing filled the room. *My work here is done.* I wanted to ravish her mouth and let her savor the taste on my tongue, but I wasn't a total asshole. I didn't want to mess up her hair and makeup on our special day.

I slipped off the bed and smiled at her, my gaze lingering between her legs as I wished I could fuck her right now.

She sat up and closed her legs. *A total lady.* I'd make her my slut in a week's time.

"Finish getting ready." I gazed in the mirror above her

dresser and fixed my tousled hair. "In a few minutes, we'll make this official, and then I'll show you what I really want to do to you."

Before leaving the bedroom, I glanced over my shoulder, taking in her frazzled expression and flushed cheeks. "Luciana, don't be late. I'll make you regret it."

"I wouldn't dream of it." She bit the corner of her bottom lip, tempting me in ways she knew nothing about. "You may have just taught me the importance of being on time."

"Girls who are on time have orgasms."

"*Women* who are on time have orgasms," she corrected me. "And in your case, it's singular, not plural anymore."

*Staking her claim. I like it.*

When I stepped out into the hallway, Sandro headed in my direction. His shocked expression gave everything away.

*That's right, your sweet little cousin is all mine to corrupt.*

I wiped my mouth with the back of my hand and winked at him as we passed in the hall. "I told you I would smooth things over with her."

*Maybe I am the marrying type, after all.*

As I made my way down the staircase decorated in lace and white lights, I found Kristina waiting for me.

"Mr. Bilotti," she said. "I see you're not keeping with traditions."

"I'm not a traditional guy." I motioned to the over-the-top wedding decorations. "You didn't hold back."

"Well, we're not really celebrating your union to my clueless niece, are we?" She smiled. "Although, I can't thank you enough for taking her off our hands."

"It's my pleasure."

"Hmm, I guess it will be." She smirked. "This celebration is more about the alliance you're creating with my family. With you on our side, how can we go wrong?"

She looked me over, like she was trying to determine if I was a worthy opponent. She'd find out soon enough, especially if she crossed me.

## CHAPTER 15

*Luciana*

When I stepped through the patio doors and entered the backyard, the idea of going through with this paralyzed me with fear. Not even the light melodic strumming coming from the harp calmed me.

There were roses everywhere. Petals even covered the water in the pool. My aunt may not have liked me, but she'd pulled out all the stops for this phony wedding.

Everyone sat in clean, white rental chairs, except my uncle, who waited to escort me down the aisle and give me to a business associate. My aunt and cousins sat prominently up front. They'd filled each row with people I didn't know. There were a few distant cousins sprinkled in for good measure.

Romero stood under a large trellis adorned with more roses. Gio was by his side, filling the role of his best man. I didn't have anyone to stand by my side. I didn't know why that bothered me. It wasn't as if this was the real deal. I would get a do-over someday. Right?

My second chance would be different in my new life. My

groom would actually want to marry me. We would have mutual friends who would celebrate us. I'd have a maid of honor to help me with my dress and hold my flowers. It wasn't too late to find that happiness. I had to hold on to the hope that one day things would be different. I wouldn't be a prisoner forever.

An unimaginable amount of sadness flooded my emotions. I sucked in a breath and held back the tears. I wouldn't cry. I wouldn't give any of them the satisfaction of crying. No matter how miserable my life was, it was my life, and I had to control it.

My uncle took my arm and linked it with his. "It's time, *bella*."

"I... I'm terrified."

"You can do this."

What if he was wrong? What if I couldn't do this? What if I couldn't will my legs to walk the length of the white runner and meet Romero under the trellis? I wanted to run away and never come back. Then I remembered the way he made me feel thirty minutes ago.

Once our eyes connected, everything else faded into the background. I walked down the aisle on autopilot, knowing none of this was traditional, despite the optics my aunt had created. Romero didn't love me. He didn't even want to marry me. He'd agreed to it, but only for his personal gain. I was the extra baggage that came with the deal. None of that seemed to matter when I met his hungry gaze, because what I saw in his eyes excited me. He wanted me like no man ever had.

I could use that to my advantage.

When I met him at the end of the walkway, my heart rate sped up. My uncle kissed my cheek and then placed my hand in Romero's. His part of the deal was done. He had given me to his rival.

My soon-to-be husband gave my hand a gentle squeeze, confusing me even further.

I stood with my back to all the people who had shown up to witness this union, nodding and repeating vows that meant nothing to me. I forced myself to go through the motions. Romero never let go of my hand. Was he trying to comfort me, or was he afraid I would bolt?

The minister said something about rings and Gio placed a silver band in my hand. Where did it come from? Did Romero buy it himself? Should I have offered to do that?

Again, I went through the motions. I spoke the words. *With this ring, I thee wed...*

When it was Romero's turn, he raised my hand between us and took off my engagement ring so he could put the spectacular matching diamond band on my ring finger. He didn't have to tell me because I already knew, but he must have recognized the unspoken question in my expression.

"It was my mother's," he whispered before putting my engagement ring back on my finger. The two rings looked fabulous together, but this wasn't the first doomed marriage they had seen.

The thought of him giving me something so sentimental made my stomach twist and I willed myself not to vomit. How could he give something so valuable to him to a woman who was only there to betray him? I silently promised myself when this was over, I would return these gorgeous treasures to their rightful owner. Maybe someday he could give them to a woman who deserved to wear them. I wasn't her.

"I present to you, Mr. and Mrs. Bilotti," the minister announced, and everyone applauded.

Romero leaned into my flushed face and gently tilted my chin up before placing a soft, chaste kiss on my lips. Not at all the heated connection I expected.

"I'm saving the real one for later," he whispered into my ear.

He turned me to face our guests, closing his hand in mine and ushering me down the aisle. A feeling of dread came over me because I wasn't the same woman I was when I woke up this morning. I was no longer a Torrio. I was a Bilotti.

Could I learn to embrace such a lie?

Bottles of champagne popped around us as people hugged and congratulated us. Romero never let me go. He held me tighter and closer when men from other families approached us. Was he being possessive or protective?

He guided me to a vacant corner of the patio and handed me a glass of champagne.

"You're the most stunning bride I've ever seen." He raised his glass. "To my beautiful wife."

He tapped his flute against mine. "May we only find happiness in the days ahead."

"Do you think we can?" I whispered, unsure of everything that was happening around me.

"We can try, Luciana." He sipped his drink. "I'm willing to do that for us. Are you?"

I pressed my lips to the rim of my glass and took a long sip. Before I had the chance to answer, Gio joined us.

"There's the newlyweds." He pulled me into a hug. "Welcome to the family."

"Thank you." I smiled.

"If my brother, who can be a colossal jerk, gives you any problems, you come to me and I'll set him straight." Gio stood beside his brother. Together, they created an intriguing duo. Tall, dark, muscular, and extremely hot in their tuxedos. "Don't let him bully you."

"Are you done?" Romero asked. "Because I've had enough of your bullshit."

"I'm done for now." Gio winked at me. "Torrio would like to take a quick meeting with us before the reception gets underway. He's in his study."

"I'll meet you there," Romero said.

"Don't take too long." Gio headed inside. "There are too many hot girls at this party, and I don't want to keep them waiting. I'm also too sober for my liking."

I laughed at Gio's light-hearted attitude. He may have looked like his older brother, but he was far less intense.

"I like him," I said.

"I don't think I've ever seen you do that."

"Do what?"

"Laugh."

"Oh, well, we haven't been around one another that often."

"It's unfortunate that it was my brother who could make you laugh and not me." He put his flute down on one of the high-top tables set up on the patio. Was he really that offended? "I won't be long."

"I'll be here."

"Can you try not to encounter another man who makes you smile for him?"

"Maybe you could try to make me smile for you." I finished my drink. "Just a thought."

"You have a smart mouth, Mrs. Bilotti." He walked toward the house. "I'm going to find something else for you to do with it."

*Promises, promises...*

While Romero was in his meeting, I spent my time

thanking guests for coming and making small talk with them. I couldn't find my cousins. They were probably with Romero. What were they talking about today of all days? Couldn't business be set aside for one day? Probably not, considering this day was one big business deal.

I walked around the side of the house as the sun was setting. They would serve dinner soon, and then I'd have to start my new life with my husband. What would that entail? Maybe I would be surprised. What if Romero and I could make it work? What if he turned out to be the husband I had dreamed about? The friend I had wished for?

*Let's be real, Lu.* How could we ever have anything good when I was starting this whole relationship on a lie?

"Mrs. Bilotti." A voice from behind jolted me from my thoughts.

When I turned to face him, I found an imposing man standing by the gate. He was tall and muscular. His black hair was pulled into a sleek ponytail, and his intriguing blue eyes pierced through me. He had a tattoo on his right hand, but the rest of his skin was covered in his tailored tux. He must have been a guest, but I didn't recognize him.

When he stepped toward me, I inched back. What if he was an enemy of my husband or my uncle? Were these things I'd have to worry about?

"How do you know my name?" I asked.

"It's my job to know your name. It's also my job to know your whereabouts at all times. But to answer your question, you are the one wearing the wedding dress, so I assume you're the bride. I also watched you marry my boss."

"You work for Romero?"

"I do." He extended his hand. "My name is Jag."

"My new guard." I shook his hand. "Romero told me."

"I followed you out here because I didn't want you to be

alone." He nodded toward the house. "There are a lot of questionable people here."

"I've lived here most of my life." I pointed toward the sky. "I like to watch the sunset from here."

"It's beautiful." He stared up at the sky. "But don't tell anyone I said that."

"It would ruin your tough reputation." I laughed at my strapping security guard enjoying the sunset. "I wouldn't dream of it."

"I see you've met your guard." Romero joined us. "And look at that. He made you laugh."

He glared at Jag.

"Oh, I didn't make her laugh. She, um..." Jag looked at me and then back to Romero. "She made herself laugh."

"Did she?" Romero pointed toward the backyard. "Go have dinner."

"Yes, boss." He hurried back to the yard as he was ordered to do.

"Why were you so mean to him?" I asked.

"You think that was mean?" He looked out at the setting sun. "I thought I told you to stop letting other men make you laugh."

"Maybe you shouldn't leave me alone so that other men have the opportunity to do such things."

When I moved toward the yard, he caught me by the wrist and turned me to face him, keeping a tight grasp on me.

"I have a warning for you, sweetheart."

"What is it?"

"As much as I find your sassy side cute, there are certain things I won't tolerate." His gaze was harsh and his jaw twitched when he clenched his teeth. "Don't make me jealous. It won't end well for anyone, especially not for the guy who makes you laugh."

"You're being ridiculous." I tried to pull out of his hold, but he wouldn't relent.

"I don't think I am."

"I haven't had much experience with men. It's been two years since I've been on a date. I married you today. Why would I want to make you jealous of one of your guys?"

"You're my wife." He tugged me closer to him and when his gaze dropped to my lips, I realized we hadn't had a real kiss yet. My lips trembled in anticipation. "I own your laugh, your smile, your tears, your body, your orgasms, your soul. I own it all."

"You can have all of it." I licked my lips. "None of it was ever really mine to begin with."

He let go of me, taking my hand in his and bringing my knuckles to his lips.

"Luciana, I said I wanted to try." He ran his thumb over my rings. "I can't do that if you don't meet me halfway."

"We should go back to the reception," I said. "Dinner is being served. They'll wonder where we are."

"I don't care what those strangers think."

"Please." I squeezed his hand. "Let's start by attending our wedding reception and we'll see where it takes us."

How could I tell him I wanted to try when I was only there to spy on him? Where would the lie end and where would we begin?

**CHAPTER 16**

*Romero*

Once I had Luciana in the back of the limo after the reception, I pulled her into my lap.

"You're not resisting?" I asked.

"I have a feeling I'd be wasting my energy if I did."

"You would be and it would only piss me off."

I ran my fingers through her soft curls, pulling pins out and tossing them on the floor until I had her hair down and wild. Twisting my fingers in her locks, I brought her mouth to mine.

"About that kiss," I whispered.

She sighed against my lips and closed her eyes as our mouths collided. I pushed my tongue between her lips, really kissing her this time. Her skin was soft and warm, and she gave into me so innocently as she let me take the lead. Her sweetness made me fucking hard. How was I supposed to be tame for her first time when I couldn't even get control of myself while kissing her?

I shifted her in my lap, hiking her dress up and placing her legs on either side of my thighs. She clung to me with such need.

She still hadn't told me she was in this with me to make this a real marriage. I wasn't sure why that bothered me. If she didn't want me as her husband, she definitely wanted me to fuck her. That I could work with.

I slipped my hand under her dress and to her center, surprised but pleased to find she was bare. I arched a brow at her. "What's this?"

"You took my panties off, remember?"

"How could I forget?"

"I didn't think you wanted me to put them back on."

"You were right."

She unbuttoned my jacket and glossed her hands over my chest, reaching for the buttons of my shirt.

I held my hands over hers, stopping her. "What are you doing?"

"Touching you."

"We should wait until we get home." I couldn't fuck her in the back of this limo like some animal. Well, I could, but that wasn't any way to take her virginity. There would be plenty of other opportunities to do her in a car.

"Why?" She ran her hands along my stomach and up the length of my chest. "What if I can't wait?"

"What if you start something you can't finish?" I raised my hips, allowing her to feel what she had already done to me. "That could be a problem."

"I don't want to wait." She lowered her hands to my belt as she pressed her lips to my jaw. "You don't either."

I sat back and let her take the lead. I wouldn't let it last long, but I was curious to see how far my little virgin could take things before she needed my help.

She fumbled with my belt and button, but eventually managed to get my zipper down. There was something enchanting about her inexperience. It had been a long time since I had been with a virgin.

*Where is she going with this?*

"Fuck," I moaned when she put her hand inside my underwear and wrapped her fingers around my length. I hadn't expected that. "You're playing a dangerous game."

"That game started the moment I said *I do*." She moved her palm up and down my shaft, glancing down between us. "Actually, I think it started in my bedroom. I can't stop thinking about what you did to me before the ceremony."

"My wedding gift."

"I want to give you a present."

I took her chin between my fingers and tilted her face up. "Get on your knees."

She stopped the motion with her hand and looked into my eyes. I saw the uncertainty in hers.

"If I can't make you smile, I'll make you gag." I guided her off my lap and onto the floor in front of me. "Let's see how far you're willing to take this."

I twisted my fingers in her hair and grabbed the base of my cock in my other hand. "Open."

"I've never done this." The panic in her voice excited me in ways she would never understand. "Not here, please."

"I told you not to start what you couldn't finish." I tugged on her hair. "Open your mouth."

She bit the corner of her bottom crimson lip before obeying my command. I guided her mouth closer to my cock and pressed the tip between her lips. Bringing her head forward, she slipped her lips halfway down my shaft and then brought her mouth back to the tip.

I sighed when she swirled her hot, wet tongue around the head of my cock. She repeated this action a few times, finding her way, but never taking me all the way. The pleasure she created was more than sufficient, but I wanted her to feel all of me. I scooted forward, forcing my dick to the back of her throat. She tried to pull away, but I held her still.

"You can do this."

She nodded.

"That's my girl." I thrust my hips forward. "Relax."

She opened wider, allowing me total access to fuck her mouth. I kept a steady rhythm as I held her hair. She rested her hands on my thighs, letting me take control. Just the way I liked it.

Propelling my hips toward her, I pushed until she gagged, but she didn't stop. She squeezed the top of my legs as she kept up with my powerful thrusts. I backed off every few seconds, giving her a chance to breathe before pushing balls deep into her mouth.

I squeezed my cock, jerking myself off in time with her mouth. My heartbeat strummed loud between my ears and pounded hard against my chest.

"Luciana, you filthy girl." This wasn't going to take much longer. I gazed down at her, tugging hard on her hair, and without warning, I came in her mouth.

She jolted back, but I held her in place, making sure she took everything I gave her.

"Don't move," I moaned as I emptied between her lips. Some of my cum seeped out and down her chin.

When I pulled out of her mouth, she pressed her lips shut.

I released her hair and then took her chin between my fingers. "You should probably swallow that."

She crinkled her adorable nose and forced down my seed. I swiped my thumb across her chin and pushed the ejaculation that had dripped there between her lips. "You missed some."

She sucked my thumb into her mouth, licking it clean.
*Quick study.*

When the limo stopped in front of our house, Luciana got off the floor and sat next to me. I pulled up my zipper and fastened my pants before cracking the window enough for me to speak to my driver.

"Leave us," I said.

He nodded and walked toward the backyard to the staff entrance of the house.

I turned to my gorgeous bride and smoothed her hair with my hand. "Are you sure you've never done that before?"

"I haven't."

"You're good at it."

"Thank you." Her lips curved upward as she lowered her gaze.

"Are you smiling?"

"I think pleasing you makes me happy." She slipped her tongue between her lips. "Who knew?"

"Well, now that I know how to make you happy, we'll be doing that often." I leaned closer and pressed my mouth to hers, kissing her with a determined purpose. "Are you ready for what comes next?"

I opened the door and got out, extending my hand for her. She hesitated, but then reached for it and clasped it in hers. I wanted her to need me. She was delicate and innocent, and all the things I wasn't.

As we walked toward our home with her hand in mine to begin our new life, a surge of possessiveness came over me. It was more than claiming her and making her mine. Of course, I wanted those things, but more than that, now that she was my wife, I had a duty to put her above all else. To protect and cherish her. Get her to trust me and, in return, I would trust her.

Could I do that? *Only time will tell.*

When we reached the front door, I scooped her in my arms and a melodious giggle escaped her lips. It was light and sexy. I'd made her laugh.

"What are you doing?" The surprise in her voice delighted me.

"Carrying you over the threshold."

"I thought we were making our own rules?" She held onto me as I brought her through the door and up the steps. "You don't seem like a traditional kind of guy."

"What? Don't all grooms give their bride oral sex right before the ceremony?"

"I don't think so."

"Pussies." I smirked as I pushed open the bedroom door.

She leered around the bedroom, admiring what my staff had prepared for us. It was decorated in soft white twinkling lights, pillar candles, and pink roses. Light music streamed through the sound system, setting the mood.

"You did this?"

"Not exactly," I admitted. "I instructed the staff to make our room romantic."

"It's beautiful."

"I wanted it to be okay for you."

"That was sweet of you." She wiggled her feet until her shoes hit the ground.

"I'm not that sweet." I set her on her feet. "I'm rough."

"Oh." She swallowed hard as she backed away from me.

"I like it hard and fast." I removed my tux jacket and tossed it on the chair. "I'm not gentle."

"I don't need you to be gentle."

I grabbed her arm and seized her toward me. She stumbled forward and slammed into my chest. "If you thought I was relentless in the back of the limo, that was nothing compared to how I can really be."

"You're going to have to be patient with me while I learn what you want and need."

*Fuck!* Why did her submission make me so aroused?

"I'm not a patient man." I kissed her jaw. "I'll make an exception tonight."

I turned her around and moved her hair to one side, running my lips along the back of her neck as I unbuttoned her dress. I ran my fingers down her spine to the dip above her backside. Her skin was like silk, soft and precious. Slipping the straps from her shoulders, I let the dress fall to the floor. As I closed the space between us, I gripped her hips and rubbed her against my rock hard cock.

"Feel what you do to me." I shifted my pelvis forward. "You made me come fifteen minutes ago but I'm ready for more."

I slid my hand to her bare sex and dragged my finger along her slit, playing with her clit.

Her sexy mouth fell open in a moan as she rested the back of her head on my chest.

"Soon, I'll be inside you." I pushed my fingers into her body. "Stretching you wide and making you scream my name. The only name that will ever fall from your lips. The only man who will ever make you feel this way."

"I want you," she whispered.

"Where do you want me, baby?" I continued to finger her. "Tell me."

"Everywhere." She turned in my arms and faced me. "On top of me, in my mouth, inside me. I want all of you."

"Be careful what you wish for." I nipped her bottom lip. "Once I start, I won't be able to stop."

"I won't ask you to stop."

I removed my bowtie from my neck and stretched it out between my hands, holding it in front of her.

She glanced down at the tie as I approached her.

I covered her eyes with the fabric, tying it into place. "I'm ready to play."

## CHAPTER 17

*L*uciana

I couldn't see Romero but having the bowtie over my eyes heightened my senses. Being around him terrified me, but it also aroused me in ways I didn't understand. When he'd pulled me into his lap in the back of the limo, something inside me had broken free. I couldn't keep my hands off him. My desire for this powerful and dangerous man took over, and nothing else mattered. There was no turning back now.

When he stepped away from me, I missed his touch. He was only a few feet from me, rustling out of his clothes. I wanted to remove the tie from my eyes and see him. All his muscles, tattoos, and skin.

He turned me away from him so he could undo the corset. His strong hands tended to the delicate material and he had it off me within seconds. A breath caught in my throat when I realized we were naked and ready to have sex. He guided me to face him, and I imagined he was studying my body. Did he like it?

I thought about when we were in the back of the limo.

How hard he was in my mouth. I'd had no idea what I was doing, but instinct had taken over and I'd fed off his primal needs. Would sex be the same? Would I know what to do? How to do it?

"You're thinking too hard." He trailed his fingers down my arm. "You're tense. It's written all over your face."

"I'm trying but I don't know what to do."

"You let me handle it."

"Okay," I whispered.

"Your aunt said you were on the pill. Is that still true?"

That was intrusive. Why didn't he ask me first?

"It doesn't matter either way," he added. "I'm fucking you without a condom."

"I am on the pill." A wave of nerves settled in my gut when I realized how real all of this was. "Is there anything I should know about where you've been?"

"Ah, Luciana, I admire that fiery spirit. As afraid as you are of me, you still find a way to try to stand up to me. It's adorable." He leaned into my face and kissed my jaw, then whispered into my ear, "Don't worry, my sexy wife. You're going to be the first woman I fuck bare."

I gasped at his admission.

"Do you know how beautiful you are?" He lifted me up in his muscular arms and placed me on the edge of the bed, kissing me long and passionately.

As I clung to his warm, naked body, lust cluttered my mind. I'd imagined what my first encounter would be like hundreds of times. What kind of guy it would be with. Never in my wildest dreams did I ever think I'd let a man so crass, domineering, and controlling take my virginity. Now that it was happening, I couldn't think of a more perfect person for the task.

He guided me up to the top of the bed and settled me

into the pillows, laying me down on the mattress. He raised my arm and secured it to the bed with what I assumed was silk. My muscles tensed when he did the same to the other.

"Don't panic." He swiped his lips across mine. "Let me lead."

"Why do you have to tie me up?"

"Can you trust me?"

"I... I don't know." I wanted to trust him, but I was a little overwhelmed at the moment.

"Can you try?"

"Yes."

"You won't regret it." He spread my legs apart and moved between them. "I know you like this."

He kissed my inner thigh before making his way to my center. He pushed his tongue inside me, licking and sucking all the right places.

I tugged against the restraints, bucking my hips into his face.

"So impatient." He laughed as he continued his exploration with his mouth. "I love the way you taste."

I settled into the pillows, trying to forget he had tied me to the bed. I'd definitely never imagined my first time like this. After a few minutes, being restrained didn't seem to matter anymore. Letting Romero take the lead was all I needed.

He flattened his hot tongue against my folds, taking his time to lick me while he pushed his fingers inside me. My nipples hardened and my insides pulsed over the stimulation. I pulled against the ropes as I raised my hips to meet his mouth. Even though my heart beat loudly between my ears, his faint laugh over my eagerness didn't go unnoticed.

"You're so smug." I curled my toes into the soft comforter.

"No, I just know what I'm doing." He tossed my leg over his shoulder, causing his fingers to slide deeper.

My arousal trickled down my thighs as he swirled the tip of his tongue along my clit. I thrust my hips forward, demanding more, and he didn't disappoint. He hurried his tempo, keeping a coordinated rhythm with his fingers and mouth. The man had mad skills.

"Oh..." A tingling sensation coursed through me as I climaxed against his face. My legs trembled and my arms ached from the restraints. When the aftershocks took over, Romero slithered up my body and reached between us, pushing his tip against my opening.

"Wait!" I panicked. "Untie me and take the blindfold off."

"You seem to think you're in charge." He shifted his hips forward, moving further inside me. "What if I want to take you like this?"

"No." I tried to wiggle my arms free, but it was no use. "Please."

"I'm going to untie you." When he removed his bowtie from my eyes, I blinked a few times, focusing on his beautiful green eyes and sexy full lips. "I need you to relax first."

"I'm scared."

"I know." He gently kissed me, allowing me to taste myself on his tongue. "I can't promise I won't hurt you, but I'll try to make it okay for you."

When he thrust his hips forward, breaking my barrier, I screamed out in response. The tears streamed down my face in hot, salty drops as he worked himself inside me. I didn't like this intrusion.

"We need to stop."

"Breathe." He reached up and untied my arms and guided me onto the bed. "It'll get better."

"When?" I sucked in a breath, resisting the urge to push him away from me.

"Maybe not tonight." He supported himself on his forearm. "I want you to take all of me."

I shook my head because I could barely handle what he'd given me now.

"Yes, Luciana." He lifted my leg and held it over his hip, forcing more of him inside me. My body stretched and responded to his swollen length. "You can do it and when you do, you'll experience all the pleasure we can share with one another."

I gripped his shoulders and took a deep breath, preparing myself to accept all of him. "Don't hold back."

"That's my girl." He grasped my leg, closed his eyes, and shoved his hips forward, moving deep inside me.

Lowering his head, he sucked my nipple into his mouth, biting and licking it. At first, the sensation was painful, but the more he licked and sucked, the more I craved. The discomfort between my legs turned into something else. I arched my back and moved my hips in time with his thrusts. The growls and heavy breathing coming from him were all the motivation I needed.

"Fuck." He sat back on his heels, taking me with him and settling me into his lap. "You're so tight around my cock."

I took his face between my hands and fiercely kissed his lips, claiming them as he wrapped his fingers in my hair, holding me close. His stubble scraped against my jaw and down my neck when he tugged and turned my head, taking control of the kiss. His mouth was rough and unforgiving, matching his forceful upward thrusts. I bounced and jerked in his lap while his fingers crushed into my waist and his teeth bit into my lips.

"I need you to turn around."

"What?" I froze because I didn't understand what he was asking. "Why?"

"Because I want more." He pulled me off his lap and turned me to face the wall. "I need to get deeper."

"Oh." I thought he wanted...

Before I had time to process, I was propelled into the headboard. I gripped the iron spindles for support.

"Romero!" I screamed when he entered me and didn't stop.

"I can't be gentle, butterfly." He grunted as he dug his fingers into my hips. "I tried, but this is how I need it. Hard, fast, and unforgiving."

"I like it," I breathed out.

"Ah, fuck!" He reached around and pushed his finger against my clit as he slammed into me from behind. "I'm so close."

"What are you doing?" I slid my hand down my stomach and placed it on top of his hand.

"Making you come." He rubbed my clit between his thumb and finger while he kept up a relentless pace with his cock.

I trembled beneath his rigid body, indulging in the way he growled in my ear.

"Luciana..." he groaned as he released his hot come inside my waiting core.

As he let go, a strong urge broke from inside me, starting in my stomach and traveling lower.

"Don't stop moving." I pushed my hips back. "I..."

"Come for me." He tugged me in an upright position, slamming my back against his muscular chest. He rolled his pelvis at a slow, easy pace, keeping a steady strum against my clit with his fingers as I came.

"I could do this all night." He kissed the back of my neck. "But you can't handle that."

He was right. I was spent, and I didn't think my body would be receptive to another assault, no matter how wonderful it felt.

Pushing me flat onto the mattress, he settled on top of me, pinning me between the bed and his rock solid form. He stayed inside me for a few minutes. Our frantic breathing slowed, and I closed my eyes, enjoying the closeness of this moment. We'd never shared anything like this before. I never expected to feel so good, so desired, so his.

When he climbed off me, I moved onto my back as he disappeared into the bathroom. I glimpsed his sexy backside, but that was nothing compared to the full frontal I received on his way back into the bedroom. *Holy fuck!*

"You like what you see?" He smirked.

"Maybe." I looked away, embarrassed that he caught me lusting after him.

He joined me on the bed with a warm, wet washcloth. "There's some blood."

"Oh." I bit my lip, mortified at the thought of him cleaning me up.

"It's natural." The way he tended to me in such a caring manner took me by surprise. "Are you okay?"

"Yes, a little sore but not horrible."

He cupped the side of my face in his hand. "Thank you for giving me that." He kissed me softly. "It took a lot of trust on your part."

"Yes." I took a breath, trying to settle my thoughts. I trusted him with my virginity. Would I trust him with my life?

"I won't take that lightly." He kissed me again. "You should rest."

"I think I'm too keyed up to sleep."

"It's been a long day." He got up from the bed and went to the walk-in closet. "Can I get you anything?"

"No."

He emerged from the closet, tugging a t-shirt over his head, covering his brawny tattooed chest. He'd put on a pair of gray sweatpants while he was in there.

"I have to go to work."

"Now?" I pulled the comforter over myself. "It's our wedding night."

"I know, sweetheart, but I've been away from my business all day." He walked toward the door, but he lingered with his back to me. "I have messages to answer and things that need my attention."

"But I thought we could..." I stopped when he turned the handle on the door.

"They'll be other nights." He turned and winked at me. "I promise."

When he left, I hopped out of bed and ran to the door, but then I stopped. *Have some respect for yourself.* Why was I chasing him? Clearly, I was no better than any other woman he'd taken to bed. His work was more important than I would ever be.

Why was I surprised? I'd seen my uncle do it my whole life. He worked all day at the firm, appeared at dinner, and then left for the evening. Some nights he'd never even bothered to come home. I'd heard rumblings of an apartment he kept in the city. He didn't sleep alone there. I wondered how Aunt Kristina could accept such a flaw in her relationship. As I got older, I told myself she deserved whatever she got for marrying a man like my uncle.

*Am I headed for the same fate? Or far worse?*

## CHAPTER 18

*Romero*

On Sunday morning, I knocked on the master bedroom door. I had an important day ahead of me and I didn't have time to put my new bride in her place.

"Luciana," I said. "We're going out in twenty minutes."

"What?" She barely opened the door as she spoke to me. "I'm not going anywhere with you."

"You don't have a choice." I pushed against the door, causing it to swing open. Her wild dark curls fell down her shoulders and over her white lace nightgown that was probably meant for our wedding night. "Be downstairs in twenty minutes."

"Or what?"

"I'll come up here and drag you down myself."

She slammed the door in my face.

It was safe to say I'd pissed her off, and we weren't even married for twenty-four hours. That had to be some sort of record.

Despite her anger, she got ready and joined me in the back of the SUV. I had to take this meeting with some international sellers. I thought I should bring my new bride along so she could see what she had gotten herself into. I didn't trust these people, but Antonio had referred them to me. Maybe that was why a knot had settled in the pit of my stomach about this meeting. Eventually, I would have to learn to trust my in-laws, but I wasn't there yet.

Normally, I didn't mind the silence. I enjoyed getting lost in my dark thoughts, but right now, I needed a distraction and her chilly reception wasn't doing much for my mood.

"Did you sleep well?" I asked.

"The bed's too big for one person." She scrolled on her phone, hardly paying attention to me.

"It's not meant for one person."

"Well, I was the only person in it last night, wasn't I?"

I unbuckled my seatbelt and moved closer to her. She inched away from me, so I gripped her thigh. She tensed under my touch as if it repulsed her. When I slid my hand under her skirt, she smacked it away.

*What the fuck?*

"I want to touch you." I squeezed her thigh harder. "Don't stop me."

"I don't want you to." She crossed her legs.

"You didn't mind last night." I spread her legs apart and pushed my hand between them, causing her to drop her phone. "If I remember, you couldn't get enough."

"Stop it." She glanced at Salvi, my driver, who had no interest in what we were doing back here. "I don't want to."

"It's his job to drive the car." I pushed my finger against her lace covered slit. "He doesn't care what we're doing."

"Don't touch me." She shoved me away and scooted to the corner of the seat.

"Don't you fucking tell me what to do." I advanced her,

trapping her between the door and my body, but she didn't look at me. "You're mine."

"No," she whispered. "I'm not a possession."

"Your uncle thinks you are. He sold you to me for an alliance that he really didn't need."

When she didn't acknowledge me, it only made me more furious and unsettled than I already was. I grabbed her hair and turned her to face me.

"Stop." She tugged at my hand, but I didn't release her.

"You don't have the luxury of saying no to me." I didn't raise my voice, but she shrank away. "If I want to fuck you right here and right now, you're going to let me do it because that's how this works."

Her eyes filled with tears that spilled down her cheeks as she trembled against me. I hated seeing her this way, but she needed to accept who I was and where her place was in this relationship.

"Do you understand?" I asked.

She nodded.

"Tell me you understand, Luciana."

She whimpered when I yanked her head back.

"Use your words."

"I understand. It's just that..."

"It's just what?" I demanded because I had very little patience this morning.

"I'm sore from last night and I don't want it to hurt." More tears leaked out of her eyes. "Please don't hurt me."

*Ah, fuck!*

"Don't cry." When I released her hair, she rubbed where I had pulled.

*I'm such an asshole.*

"This is exactly why I left you last night." I wiped the tears from her cheeks. "I didn't trust myself to leave you alone. I would have fucked you all night if I had stayed. You couldn't have handled that. It was better for me to leave, so I did."

"You could have stayed with me."

I could have done a lot of things, but I did what I wanted. I wasn't used to answering or explaining to anyone. When I moved back into my seat, she curled up in the corner of hers and stared out the window. She looked so small and fragile. Sometimes I forgot she was only twenty-two and had little experience in this world. She wasn't used to men, especially one like me.

I clenched my fist in my lap, swearing to myself I wouldn't be like my father. I had watched him beat the shit out of my mother so many times when I was a kid. That morning I found her on the bathroom floor, it was too late. I couldn't...

"I'm sorry," I whispered, but if she heard me, she didn't respond. Could I blame her? I would have ignored me too. I took her virginity last night and then I left her alone and unsupported. I didn't explain why. She must have felt abandoned. This was why I wasn't meant to be a husband.

Before I could fuck things up anymore, Gio called my cell.

"What?" I answered.

"Where are you?"

"We're on our way."

*"We're?"*

"Luciana is with me." I should have left her at home. "Is that a problem?"

"I don't know if it's a good idea," he said. "These sellers are rough."

"Rougher than me?"

"Look, they've already started negotiations and I can tell you you're not going to like what they have to offer."

"Wonderful." Why couldn't things ever go as planned? "What are they saying?"

"It's not what they're saying as much as what they're charging."

"We set the price."

"They want to change the terms."

"At the last minute?" I didn't have the patience for this. "Are they offering anything special that would make this eleventh hour change acceptable?"

"Same product at a higher price. I think we should walk away."

"And miss all the fun?" I asked. "Do we outnumber them?"

If I had the upper hand, I had nothing to worry about. I wasn't known to negotiate with people who were in the business of trying to screw me over. They were going to learn real quick who was in charge.

"We have men on the ground they don't know about in case there's trouble. I can't say for sure if they have other soldiers with them. I have security doing a sweep. Right now, it looks like there are only four of them."

"There won't be four when I'm done." I glanced at Luciana, who was still staring out the window.

*What is she thinking? Hell, what am I thinking? I can't let her distract me.*

"Make sure we have a forceful presence when I arrive. If they have more men in hiding, some of them will come out."

"They'd be pretty stupid if they showed up alone."

"Most of them are." I ended the call.

We arrived at the location nestled in the woods. It was desolate and perfect for such a business meeting, especially with its proximity to the river. When the car stopped, I reached down and retrieved Luciana's phone from the floor. I scooted closer to her, grateful she couldn't move away from me, but she refused to face me.

"We're here." I undid her seatbelt. "Can you at least appear that you like me?"

"That's a big ask."

As meek as she was, she had a spunky streak.

"Here." I held out her phone.

"Thank you." She turned her body toward me and took her phone. "Why am I here?"

"Because my associates need to believe the alliance between me and your family is strong and real. If you're with me, they can't deny you're my wife." I cupped her face in my hand. "You don't need to say anything. I only need your presence."

She gazed into my eyes, as if she was trying to process what I had just said. I wished I could get inside her mind and hear what she thought. It probably wouldn't be anything good concerning me, but at least I would know.

"Okay," she whispered.

"I have no interest in hurting you." I leaned into her and kissed her hard, taking my time to explore her mouth with my tongue. When I pulled back, she gasped for air, her eyes wide with shock. Maybe it was desire. It was difficult to read her.

Salvi opened my door.

"Show time." I winked at Luciana before sliding out and extending my hand for her. The uneasy expression plastered all over her face didn't go unnoticed, but she took my hand.

Gio met us at the car, not at all his carefree and usual goofy self. His tense muscles strained under his forearms, to his biceps, along his neck, and to his jaw. He gave Luciana a small smile before focusing his attention on me. His demeanor did nothing to settle me down.

"This meeting is a waste of time." He motioned to the four men standing in the distance.

They wore black suits and dull black shoes. What kind of man didn't take the time to polish his shoes? If they thought they could get one over on me, their appearance was the last thing they should be concerned with.

"They didn't come here to negotiate a price," Gio said. "They want us to pay double for the merchandise."

"In what universe?"

I sighed in frustration because I never would have met with these scumbags if Torrio hadn't referred them and now they were fucking trying to fleece me?

"Keep her close to you." I nudged Luciana in my brother's direction. "Are our men in place?"

"They're ready for an ambush," Gio said. "They're prepared."

"An ambush?" Luciana inched back toward the car, but Gio took her arm in his hand. "I thought this was a business meeting."

"It is." I headed toward the four sellers, ready to state my terms. "Watch how I do business."

There was only one way to deal with people like this. In my business, someone at the top of the food chain could never show weakness. These sellers knew my terms before I arrived. We set the details, and this meeting was supposed to be an exchange of money and product. For them to change the conditions now was a show of disrespect. If I allowed that, others would follow. I would gain a reputation that I could be worked over. *Fuck that.* I didn't spend years becoming the man I was today for these four nobodies to come into my territory and try to fuck me over.

"Mr. Bilotti," the first guy I approached said. From my research, he was their chief negotiator. "How nice of you to finally join us."

"My brother has filled me in on what I've missed." I stared them down, noting the cheap suits they wore. If a man didn't take pride in his appearance, how could I trust his intentions? "Needless to say, I'm not happy."

"I'm sorry to hear that but after some consideration, I've decided that the price you asked for was below asking and I'm not willing to let the product go for so little."

"I see." The price I had offered was more than generous. "Perhaps with you out of the way, your associates might feel differently. More inclined to see things may way."

"I'm sure I don't understand what you mean," he said.

"Don't you?" I clenched my fist, hauled my hand back, and punched him in the face. Blood spilled from his nose before he hit the ground with a loud thud. I stepped forward and looked down at the pathetic heap beneath my feet.

He pressed his hand to his nose in a futile attempt to stop the bleeding.

"I don't like when people waste my time."

## CHAPTER 19

*Luciana*

I turned away when Romero began kicking the man in his stomach and ribs.

"Let me go." I tried to pull away from Gio. "Please."

I couldn't take the sound of Romero's foot connecting with the man's bones. At some point, his victim stopped making any noise.

"Romero's got it." Gio held me still. "Don't worry."

*Worry? What kind of person hurts another so violently? My husband, that's who.* My uncle and cousins kept me away from these types of situations. Whether that was an accident or by design, I didn't care. Right now, I wanted to leave.

The man appeared lifeless, too still. Romero had beaten him so severely and swiftly that the other men he was with didn't even react or try to stop him. Maybe they were as shocked as I was.

Romero moved to the second guy, drew his gun from the back of his waistband, and held it on the man who didn't even flinch.

*What is wrong with these people? Who does business like this first thing on a Sunday morning?*

"I hope you're smarter than your friend." Romero waved his gun around, causing the last two men to take out their guns. "Does our original deal stand?"

"Fuck you," the man said. "You get the deal my associate offered. Out of respect you should take it."

"I don't accept that." Romero glared at the two men who didn't seem at all sure of what to do. "We negotiated a price. I want the merchandise, but I won't pay anymore than I've offered. I'm a fair man, so I'll give you an opportunity to reconsider."

"You're out of luck," the man said.

"It's not me who is out of luck," Romero responded.

A flash, followed by a booming noise, made me jump back. I covered my ears with my hands and buried my head in Gio's shoulder, shaking against him. A loud thud, screams, and rustling surrounded me. Gio pulled his gun out with one hand and held me close to him with his other.

"What the fuck?" A voice filled with shock interrupted the chaos. "Are you crazy?"

"Most people would say so," Romero said.

I peeked out from Gio's grasp to find everyone armed and ready to shoot. They must have come from the woods when I wasn't looking. Romero had shot the second man, and now the third and fourth men had their guns trained on him. All the Bilotti soldiers were ready to shoot at any given moment. More men came out of the woods, rushing the scene armed and ready for battle against the two men who now were tasked with defending themselves from Romero's wrath.

"You could try to shoot me, but you better not miss," Romero told them. "But if you take that shot, I can guarantee you won't make it out of here alive. Do you know how I know that?"

Neither of them answered.

"Because these two scumbags," he said, pointing to the dead bodies at his feet, "left you out-numbered and in a horrible position. Not a very good business strategy. Either they are, or should I say, *were,* extremely stupid or they underestimated me. It doesn't really matter now though, does it?"

"What do you want?" One man stepped forward.

All the Bilotti soldiers, with their fingers on the triggers, moved closer to Romero. Gio kept his gun up, but he pushed me to stand behind him.

Like that was going to protect me if they started shooting.

"What I came for," Romeo said. "And you better give it to me."

*Please, give him what he wants. I can't watch anyone else die.*

"And then some. You give me a sweet enough deal, the both of you are going to walk out of here a hell of a lot richer than you would have if you had to split the profits four ways." He laughed. "Looks like I did you a favor."

When the men conferred with one another, they looked as if they were arguing. These had to be the dumbest arms dealers in the world.

"Get it together," Romero warned. "You get one shot at this. If you fuck it up, you're not walking out of here at all."

"We'll take the initial price we agreed on before this meeting," the taller of the two said. "We'll throw in two extra pieces and we'll cover the price to transport it to you."

"That's better." Romero motioned for everyone to lower their weapons.

The tension dissipated and everyone was doing business

again like nothing had happened. Two men were dead because of my husband, the same man who had purchased illegal weapons to do God knew what with.

What the hell did I get myself into?

I leaned against the car as the men finished their negotiations. My breathing slowed down to an acceptable pace and my heart didn't feel like it was going to pop out of my chest. At some point, Jag stood by my side and Gio joined Romero, but I didn't say anything to my new guard. He must have sensed I didn't want to talk, so he kept me at arm's length and let me be. He was the strong, silent type, and that worked for me.

I didn't want to be around any of these people, and now I was realizing if I ever got out of this mess, I had no desire to go back to my family. They had willingly put me in the middle of all of this, so I could bring them information like what I'd witnessed in these woods. I had half a mind to tell them I had nothing for them. But who would I be protecting? Romero and his men? I was stuck in the middle of a deadly game. One I didn't know what the rules were.

Was it my uncle's concern that sleazy dealers tried to fleece Romero? Was that the type of information he wanted? Was I supposed to know the exact meeting location? The names of the dead men? What Romero purchased? How was I supposed to figure all of that out when I was scared for my life?

Romero and Gio headed back to the car as the others loaded into their SUVs. I didn't know what was more disturbing: that I'd watched the man I'd married only twenty-four hours ago murder two people in cold-blood or that he appeared so calm and together after murdering said people.

"My work is finished here." He pressed his hand to the small of my back. "We can go home."

"I want to ride with Gio," I said.

"No." He guided me toward his car. "You're my wife and you'll leave with me."

"I don't want to go with you." I stared at Gio, practically begging him to let me go with him. The lesser of two evils and all. "Please."

"I think it's best if you go with Romero," Gio said. "I'll see you back at the house."

He turned and walked toward his car, leaving me with Romero who didn't look very pleased with me.

"Get in the car." He opened the door and shoved me inside. "What were you thinking?"

He joined me in the backseat, so I slid all the way to the far end.

"Why would you want to go with my brother?"

"Why do you think?" I turned and faced the window because I was too confused and upset over what I had seen. "I don't want to talk to you."

"What else is new?"

He took out his phone and buried himself in his work. I gazed out the window, wondering how badly it would hurt if I jumped out the door and made a run for it. I probably wouldn't get that far. I'd most likely get killed or injure myself. If that didn't happen, Romero would carry me back to the car and lecture me on why I shouldn't have tried to escape in the first place.

*I'm fucking doomed.*

I glanced over my shoulder to find him still lost in his phone, and I was glad he honored my request to leave me alone.

I studied his profile. A light dusting of stubble grazed his jawline. Every once in a while, he tightened his jaw and the lines in his forehead creased when he concentrated on whatever had him so intrigued by his phone.

A few minutes ago, I was terrified of him. But now, in the quiet, as I observed him, I wanted to learn more about him. What made a man do the things he did? I didn't believe he was born a killer. He was blessed with incredible looks, stunning eyes, an athletic build, and amazing bone structure. He knew how to wear a suit, too. There was an intelligence about him. And, his speech, when he wasn't using the f-bomb every other word, was articulate and well thought out.

He could have become anything in the world. Why a gangster?

"Are you done staring at me?" He didn't look up from his phone. "What has you so fascinated?"

"Nothing." I returned my attention back to the window.

I hated to admit it, but I was fascinated with him. Scared, intimated, and fearful of my life, but intrigued. I wasn't naïve enough to believe I was the woman who was going to change him, but if I had to be his wife, what was the harm in getting to understand him? What else did I have to do?

Spy on him. I closed my eyes and tried not to think about the reason I'd married him. After last night, my mission didn't seem like a business arrangement. Having a physical relationship complicated matters, but I couldn't help myself. I wanted him to touch me, to make me feel the things he had last night.

I shifted in my seat when I recalled how he had handled me. How rough and dominating he had been with me, but at the same time, he could be tender and caring.

*What are you doing?*

I was here for one reason, and one reason only, and that

wasn't to save Romero. It was the opposite. His meeting in the woods had provided me with my first act of betrayal. It would please my uncle when I gave him the details of my morning.

But could I live with myself?

**CHAPTER 20**

*Romero*

As soon as we pulled into the driveway, Luciana practically lunged out of the car and ran into the house. It surprised me that she hadn't tried to jump out while we were still moving. I shouldn't have brought her. All it did was upset her. But now she could see me for the monster I was.

Gio wasn't far behind us as I walked into the house. Luciana stormed up the stairs without even looking at us.

"How was that car ride home?" Gio followed me into my study. "Did you kiss and make up?"

"What do you think?" I sat down at my desk.

"I think your bride might not be cut out for this life. I think her uncle pawned her off on you in exchange for something bigger. I would say you got the short end of the stick, but she's so beautiful and innocent. You could make it work."

"What is it with you and my wife?" I had to let go of what had happened in the woods, but when Luciana had asked if she could ride with Gio, I'd wanted to kill my brother. It wasn't his fault, but knowing she trusted him more than she did me didn't sit well at all.

"What's that supposed to mean?" He poured us a drink and set the glasses down on my desk. "She was terrified today. She saw you kill two people. Do you honestly think she was ready for that?"

"I fucked up."

"I'll say." He sat on the sofa across from me. "You knew that meeting had the potential to blow up. You're not even married a day and you're exposing her to shit like that? What's wrong with you?"

"I wasn't thinking." I wouldn't have brought her if I had known how little she really knew of our lifestyle. "I don't understand. She's not new to this life."

"You're not the same as her uncle and her cousins." He glanced out the window. "Your methods are unorthodox."

"She grew up in our world. How could she not know what we do? How we do it? Even if she'd never witnessed it, she had to have heard things. Read things. She can't be that oblivious."

Our father never hid his business from Gio and me. We learned from an early age how shit was handled. That was why we were so fucking ruthless. We knew how to survive. If that bastard gave us anything, it was the skills to make it in this cruel world.

"We knew what was what," I said.

"Because we were next in line. Heirs to this bloody throne. Luciana isn't even Torrios' kid. He has three sons. He didn't need to clue her in on what was happening."

"Then why bring her in now?"

"I told you before, that made little sense to me." He finished his drink. "We moved too fast on that one."

Gio was right, but what could I do about it now? I took

Giancarlo's advice and made an alliance with a potential enemy. I married Luciana, and I intended to keep those vows. Until death do us part whether she liked it or not.

"We need to make sure the scene is scrubbed." I couldn't make any more mistakes today. "There can't be any evidence that we were there. Understand?"

I sipped my vodka

"It's already being taken care of," Gio said. "Our cleaners are there now. No one will ever suspect anything. As long as the two you let live don't say anything, that is."

"They won't." I got up and headed for the door because I couldn't focus on our conversation until I took care of the situation upstairs. "They scored a lucrative deal today."

"Where are you going?"

"To check on my wife. I'll be back soon." I headed down the hall.

"Maybe you should leave her alone?" Gio stood in the doorway.

"I should but I won't."

I hurried up the steps and to the master bedroom, but when I reached the open doorway, I stopped. No punch in the gut could have hit me harder than seeing her small body shaking in the center of that huge bed. She was curled up in a ball, with her face in her phone. Her tears stabbed at my heart. What the hell? Why did I care?

She stopped texting and wiped her face when she realized I was there.

"I don't want to talk to you," she said. "I don't have anything to say."

"I shouldn't have brought you with me today." I entered the room and sat on the edge of the bed. "That was a mistake."

"Why did you?"

"I thought you could handle it."

"You thought I could handle watching you murder two men like it was nothing to you? How could you do that?"

"It meant nothing to me." I stopped feeling a long time ago. I had to if I wanted to make a name for myself. "It was business."

"How can you say that?"

"I'm good at reading people. Those men would have done the same to me if given the chance. I never let anyone get the chance. That's why I have everything I have. That's why I am who I am."

"That's who you are? The same man I let touch me last night? The same man I let take my..." She started crying again. "You were wrong. I couldn't handle it."

"This is who you married, Luciana." I threw my hands in the air because I was at a loss for words. "What did you think it was going to be like? Roses and white picket fences? You know that doesn't happen in our world. We have guards and security gates for a reason. You lived in it long enough. It has surrounded you for years."

"No." She closed her eyes and shook her head. "Not like this. My uncle isn't like you. He wouldn't do that."

"You don't think so?"

"I know he isn't a legitimate businessman, and he does questionable things." She sat up and leaned against the headboard. "Things I don't want to know about. What you did today was... horrible."

Once I took out my phone and showed her the evidence, her illusion would be shattered forever. Why should I let her think the precious Torrios were any better than me?

"Look." I held out my phone and showed her a picture of a man who had been beaten beyond recognition. His jaw and nose were shattered and he was so bloody, his eyes weren't visible in the photo. "Do you think he could do that?"

She gasped and shoved the phone back at me.

"That's what was left of a man who tried to encroach on Torrio territory. That's what happens when a person tries to take what doesn't belong to him."

"He didn't do that," she mumbled. "He couldn't."

"He definitely could, but in this case, one of the cousins you seem to idolize could."

She was so easy to hurt. I could see the heartbreak in her eyes, in her soul. The darkness inside my soul relished in hurting her. Misery loved company, and she needed to know where she came from and who she agreed to spend the rest of her life with. It was better she knew. She wouldn't be so upset if she didn't believe what I was saying wasn't true.

"What kind of men do you think we are? We're all the same. We all do what we have to do to survive. We're no saints."

She scurried off the bed and ran into the bathroom, covering her mouth with her hand. She barely made it to the toilet before vomiting. I followed her as she wretched and gagged until there was nothing left in her system. Taking a washcloth, I held it under the cool water in the sink. I wrung it out and handed it to her.

"Can you leave me alone?" She reached up and took the cloth from me. "I want to be alone."

"I'm giving you what you want because this is new to both of us." I stepped out of the bathroom. "But you can't keep hiding from me. Eventually, you're going to have to act like my wife."

I didn't wait for her to respond. She probably wouldn't have said anything, anyway. I joined my brother back in the study, feeling no better than I had when we'd first arrived home.

"How did it go?" Gio asked.

"She threw up."

"Why?"

"I showed her this." I waved my phone at him as I finished my drink.

"What the fuck is wrong with you?" He poured us another round. "Don't you think she had enough trauma today?"

"She needs to learn where she came from. I can't have her thinking I'm some fucking killer, and they are upstanding attorneys."

"Why does it matter?"

"It just does." I stared out the window, trying to process my thoughts. Why was it so important to me to gain Luciana's approval? Why did I care if she hated me? "I think you're right. Something is off."

"What do you mean?"

"Like you said, they kept Luciana out of this business her whole life and now they've thrust her into a world she can't possibly survive in. If they wanted an alliance between us, wouldn't they have prepared her for what that entailed?"

"What are we going to do about it?"

"I have one of our top guys investigating, but I need you on it. I don't trust anyone more than I trust you. Whatever you find won't be compromised."

I took a sip of my drink, closing my eyes when the burning sweet liquid coated my throat. It reminded me of my wife. She was sweet and innocent, but she could set my world ablaze in a matter of minutes, if I let her.

Would I?

"What do you need me to do?" Gio asked.

"You need to dig deep. I want to know everything there is to know about Luciana. Anything and everything you can find out about her, I want it in my hands."

"I'll see what I can get."

"Her parents. The day she came to live with her uncle. Any friends she has. I want to know why that bitch Kristina hates her so much. Find the history and we'll find the answers. If Luciana is a disposable member of that family, I want to know why. Their loss could be our gain."

"What if you don't like what I find?"

"Anyone who is trying to bring us down will be sorry."

*And I do mean anyone...*

## CHAPTER 21

*Luciana*

It had been several days since the meeting in the woods. Romero went about his business, leaving me alone with my thoughts. He went out often and came home late at night. As far as I could tell, he slept downstairs. Part of me was relieved he hadn't tried to approach me, but another part, a tiny part, was disappointed. I wasn't even sure why his avoidance of me hurt. It wasn't as if we had anything real.

My uncle was pleased with the information I had given him about Romero's meeting. I didn't realize how low it would make me feel when I answered his questions and revealed as many details as I could remember about that awful experience. What could Uncle Antonio gain from my information? I didn't have any names, and I didn't know the details of the negotiations. At the end of the conversation, he told me I had done an excellent job, and he looked forward to hearing what else I could find out. I didn't want to have to do that ever again, but I didn't have a choice.

As I made my way to the kitchen, the rustling of dishes

and pans piqued my curiosity. No one was ever in the kitchen at this time of the morning. I usually hustled in and grabbed a yogurt and a bottle of water before hurrying back upstairs so no one could see me. And, when I said *no one*, I meant Romero. Maybe it was my fault he had been staying away from me. I wasn't doing an excellent job of making myself seen.

When he left the house around three each day, I came out of my room and went downstairs. I enjoyed sitting on the back patio and reading. I stayed out there for hours, appreciating the beautiful landscaping and the warm summer air.

Today was already starting out differently. Romero should be in his office, ensconced in his work. Gio's car wasn't in the driveway, so I assumed he wasn't here yet. I should have turned around and went back upstairs, but I wanted to see who was in the kitchen. What was the saying about curiosity and the cat?

I stood in the doorway of the grand kitchen mesmerized by a shirtless Romero in blue jeans and bare feet making breakfast. I'd never seen him look so relaxed.

"Good morning, Luciana," he said without looking up from the pan of French toast. "Come in and join me."

I hesitated, but he gazed up and I caught a glimpse of his black eye and swollen lip. Without thinking, I moved forward as if I meant to tend to him. Ignoring his personal space, I stood by the stove and with a shaky hand, touched the bruise under his eye.

"It's nothing." His gaze dropped to my lips.

"It doesn't look like nothing." I traced the bump with my fingertip. "Does it hurt?"

"You should see the other guy." He winked and pointed to the kitchen island. "Sit down."

"You can cook?" I took a seat at one of the stools. The counter was set with juice, coffee, and plates for two.

"When I have to." He plated the French toast. "It occurred to me you haven't been eating since moving in here."

"I eat."

"Barely." He arched a brow at me. "I'm hiring a cook. I can't have you withering away, and I have a feeling you don't cook or else you would have attempted it over the past few days instead of sustaining off yogurt and water."

"I haven't been hungry." My nerves had been in overdrive since I'd found out I would marry him. They hadn't returned to normal. Now, they were much worse than before I'd said, *I do.* "I never learned how to cook."

We had people to do that and my aunt wasn't the maternal type, so she didn't teach me anything. I didn't think she knew how to do anything domestic. My uncle paid people to do everything.

"Do you want to learn how to cook?"

"Are you offering to teach me?" The cinnamon scent of the toast made my mouth water. "This smells delicious."

He sat next to me.

"Eat. I don't think I'd have the patience to teach anyone to cook." He splashed some creamer into his coffee. "I was thinking the person I hired to cook for us could give you lessons if you wanted."

"Maybe." What else did I have to do around here? I sipped the orange juice, trying to decide if his offer was a nice gesture or one from a man who expected me to cook for him. "Where did you learn how to cook?"

"My mother." When he cut into his toast, bananas and blueberries spilled out. "Don't let your food get cold."

"You stuffed it."

"I like fruit."

"So do I." I drizzled some syrup over my plate. "How old were you when your mother passed away?"

"Thirteen." He winced when he put the coffee mug to his swollen lip. "Eat."

I took a bite of the sweet bread. *Wow!* He definitely didn't need me to cook for him. "Did your mom used to make this for you?"

"Jag says you like to read." His abrupt change of subject alerted me that his mother was off-limits. "He said you sit outside for hours."

"It's beautiful out there. Very peaceful. It's easy to get lost in a good book." *Again, what else did I have to do?* "I didn't realize Jag was watching me."

"It's his job to watch you."

"It's a little creepy." I took another bite of my breakfast. "What happened to your face?"

"Someone took a few shots at me but that's as far as it got."

"Why would anyone provoke you?"

"I thought the same thing." He shrugged. "Some people are stupid but it won't happen again."

I didn't have to wonder why it wouldn't happen again. We ate in silence for a few minutes, but for some reason, I couldn't seem to keep quiet. The thought of his mother teaching him how to cook when he was a child made me believe there was once an innocence about him. One that was taken away. Did that happen after she died?

"Why did you choose this life?" I asked.

"You're full of questions this morning, aren't you?"

"I'm curious."

"If you eat your breakfast, I'll answer a few questions." He took another sip of his coffee. "Or at least, I'll try to."

"I'm getting full."

"Finish what's on your plate." He gestured toward my half-eaten breakfast. "This life chose me."

"I don't believe that," I said.

"Why not?"

"After your father died—"

"He was murdered," he corrected.

"After he was murdered, you walked away. You could have kept on walking. No one forced you into this life."

"That's easy for you to say, but I had my reasons."

"What were they?" I picked up a grape and popped it in my mouth. "I'm eating."

"I can't go into every reason, but I needed to prove to myself and my father's associates that I didn't need his territory. I didn't want what he built. I wanted to do it on my own."

"Wouldn't it have been easier to assume his role?"

"No." He set his fork down. "That would have put a target on my back."

"I know nothing about this business and I'm fine with that, but you still haven't said why you didn't walk away completely. You and Gio could have started over and been anything you wanted to be. Why didn't you?"

"Your question proves that you don't know anything about this business. If you did, you would understand that no one truly walks away and lives to tell about it."

*No one? Did he mean me?* My stomach churned at the thought of being stuck in this world forever. As each day passed, my options seemed to grow slimmer. I had to work for my uncle to get what he needed, but I also had to learn how to live as Romero's wife. Neither man would protect me in the end. They weren't capable of it.

"Thank you for breakfast. It was superb." I stood and

reached for my plate, but Romero grabbed my arm and tugged me to him.

My heart rate sped up when he traced his finger along my jaw and to my lips. My gut told me to run, but I couldn't move. I didn't want to run away from him. I wanted to be closer to him. There was a deep desire to allow him to do whatever he wanted to me. I accepted this was exactly where I wanted to be.

His battered face somehow made him even more appealing. He looked like a sexy boxer who had won a championship. Knowing his opponent was already six feet under should have terrified me, but a small part of me was glad he'd taken care of the person who had hurt him.

"Did you think your breakfast was free?" He trailed his hand down the side of my dress, stopping at my hip.

"I... You're teasing me." I wasn't sure how I knew, but there was something playful in his expression.

"I made you smile." He kissed me softer than I expected. "But I do what to fuck you, so if we're done with eating and the interrogation, I'd like to get on with the fucking portion of the morning."

He slipped his hands under my dress and tugged on either side of my panties, sliding them down my legs.

"Right here?" I stepped out of my underwear and glanced around the kitchen.

"Trust me." He unbuckled his belt and unbuttoned his pants. "We're not going to make it to the bedroom."

"But Gio? Salvi? Jag?" I focused on the windows that surrounded the entire kitchen. "All the others. They'll see us."

"I don't care." He lowered his zipper and pushed his pants and boxer briefs over his hips. When he lifted me on top of him, I wrapped my legs around his waist. His impressive erection pushed against my stomach. "I want you."

He unbuttoned the front of my dress, revealing my white lace bra.

"This is hot." He popped open the front clasp of the bra, freeing my breasts. "That's hotter."

He lowered his mouth to my nipple and swirled his tongue around it, forcing it to peak under his hot breath. When he sucked on it, I shifted my hips, pushing into his length. The dampness between my legs intensified with each of my movements.

"You ready for me?" He grabbed his cock in one hand and guided me up with the other. "Fuck me."

"I don't... How?"

"Like this." He pressed the tip against my entrance, pushing on my shoulder and easing me onto him. He grasped my waist in his strong hold and directed me up and down. "Perfect."

"Oh." I closed my eyes and lost myself in the pleasure we created. His thick shaft entered me at the most precise angle.

"You're gorgeous." He twisted his fingers in my hair and pushed my lips to his, kissing me roughly as I moved up and down. When he trailed his lips down my neck and to my throat, I clenched around him and grabbed the back of his chair for more leverage. Raising my hips, I slammed down, engulfing him in my wet heat.

"Is this good?" I asked.

"This is better than good." He tugged my head back and scraped his teeth along my neck. "It's fantastic."

He met me thrust for thrust, taking control and rocking me faster and harder. The more he yanked my hair and dug into my hip, the wetter I became. The pulsing between my legs escalated, and I unraveled quicker than I expected.

"Romero," I cried out, grasping the back of the chair. I released, collapsing against him, shuddering over and over.

I reveled in his possessive hold, breathing in his woodsy scent.

"My turn." He lifted me off his lap and forced me against the island, bending me over. As my arms shot out in front of me, dishes and glasses crashed to the floor, but that didn't deter him. He rammed his cock all the way in and set a relentless pace inside me. I stretched my arms out and flattened my palms against the cold granite, trying to steady myself, but it was useless. His thrusts were far too violent and demanding, so I pressed the side of my face into the counter and focused on the way he made me feel. Alive, desired, his...

He wasn't gentle, but that didn't matter. He moaned with each shift forward, losing himself inside me. The deeper he took me, the more I wanted.

"You're so fucking tight around my cock." He slammed into me, jerking me forward. "I'm going to come."

"Romero." I clenched around him as my stomach muscles tightened and I teetered on the edge of insanity again.

"Scream for me." He bit down on my shoulder hard enough to make me cry out as he shot his warmth into me.

"Oh, God!" I moaned as my legs shook beneath me and another intense, long orgasm took over my body.

He slumped on top of me, running his hand along the back of my thigh as we settled down. He kissed where he had bitten me, swiping his tongue along the sore area. Neither of us said anything but having him this close to me, touching me and holding me, seemed right.

"I'm sorry about all the questions before." I didn't know what made me apologize for wanting to get to know the man I had married.

"It's okay." He placed his hands over mine. "I'm not used to answering to anyone."

"I want to get to know you better."

"In small doses, baby." He kissed the side of my neck before turning me around and staring into my eyes. "I don't trust easily but with you I can try."

A pang of guilt settled in my heart. He can't trust me. I wasn't worthy of it. I never would be. There wasn't anything I could do about that now, but I could try, too.

"You can sleep in our bed tonight." The heat rose in my cheeks over my bold invitation, so I looked away from him. "I mean, if you want to."

"Luciana." He lifted my chin and his normal stern gaze appeared softer, more forgiving. "I definitely want to."

**CHAPTER 22**

*R*omero

The past few days were going better between my wife and me.

*My wife?* That was getting easier to accept with each new day.

She was still afraid of me. She startled easily, especially when she didn't expect me to come into a room where she was. Her anxiousness put me on edge, but I hoped she would learn to get used to me.

She hadn't seen her family since she'd moved in, so I invited her aunt and uncle to visit us. It was more of a business meeting, but it would give me a chance to observe them and see how they interacted with the new Mrs. Bilotti.

When I came into the bedroom, I found Luciana in the walk-in closet, pulling out several of the dresses I'd bought her when she came to live here. She frantically tossed them on the bed.

"What are you doing?" I asked.

"Sandro texted me and told me he and his parents are on their way here." She held up a dark blue halter dress in front of her and studied herself in the mirror. "Why didn't you tell me they were coming?"

"That's what I'm doing now." I sorted through the pile of dresses on the bed, settling on the light green one. "Wear this one. It's sexy."

I handed it to her.

"Sexy isn't what I'm going for." She picked out a black dress that looked more like she would be attending a funeral and not tea with her family. "This is more appropriate."

"Do I have to remind you what happened the last time you didn't wear the dress I wanted you to wear?" I took the black one from her and threw it on the chair by the window. "Wear the green one."

"Why did you invite them here?"

"I thought you'd like a visit." I checked my hair in the mirror and straightened my tie. "You haven't seen them since the wedding."

"That wasn't that long ago."

"You're used to seeing them every day. Don't you miss them?"

"I miss Sandro and maybe Rocco, but I didn't really interact with my aunt and uncle that often."

"What about Vincent?" The oldest Torrio was the only one I viewed as a threat. I could negotiate with the others, but Vincent was a tougher sell. There was word on the street that he was looking to bring the Torrios into the twenty-first century by expanding their territory and business ventures. My sources told me he wasn't totally on board with this alliance, but he would never go against his father's wishes.

"He's like a protective older brother." She went into the bathroom with the green dress. "We aren't that close."

"You haven't spoken to him since the wedding?"

"No."

"How about Rocco?"

"A few times. Why?"

"You text an awful lot and no offense, but you don't have any friends, so I'm wondering who gets all of your attention?"

"It's mostly Sandro." She moved around the bathroom, digging in her makeup bag. "I miss him. He's my friend."

"He's your cousin." I put on my watch and checked the time, making sure we would be downstairs when her family arrived.

"He's the closest thing I have to a friend."

That statement bothered me. I wanted to be her friend. The one she relied on and texted when she was lonely. I wanted to be the only man in her life. Didn't she know that?

When she emerged from the bathroom, I looked her over. The dress was stunning, but this woman would look good in a sack. Her perky breasts filled out the top of the low neckline, revealing enough of her cleavage to make me hard.

"Well?" She spun around. "Do you like it?"

"I love it." I pulled her toward me. "I can't wait to rip it off you."

She twisted her hair around her finger and bit her bottom lip. "Is that all you think about?"

"Yes." I wrapped my arms around her waist. "It's your fault I'm aroused all the time. You're hot. I had no idea how much I would enjoy living with you."

She lowered her gaze and her complexion glowed a soft pink.

"Don't be embarrassed." I brushed my lips across hers. "You're beautiful."

"Thank you." She looked down at the dress. "For the clothes, too. I was overwhelmed after the wedding, and I never thanked you for all the new stuff. It was thoughtful of you."

"It's nothing." I released her from my hold. "I wanted you to have some new things to go with your new life."

I reached into my pocket and took out a credit card. "This came for you today. It took a few days for it to get here but it's yours."

"What is it?"

"A credit card." I gave it to her. "Use it for whatever you want."

She looked at it, her brow wrinkled as if she might be confused. "This is mine?"

"You are *Luciana Bilotti*, are you not?"

"Why are you giving me a credit card?"

"Because I'm your husband and I take care of you now."

"I can support myself." She gave me back the card. "I have money."

"Don't insult me." I tried not to lose my temper. Why did she make everything a bigger deal than it had to be? "I've seen your bank account statement. You don't have that much money. Your cheap uncle didn't pay you much to file his papers."

"He gave me a monthly allowance and paid for anything I needed."

"So, then it shouldn't be an issue that I'm taking that over." I set the card on the dresser. "Use it or don't. It's there if you need it."

"I didn't mean to offend you." She stepped away from me, blowing out a frustrated breath.

"What's the fucking problem, Luciana?"

*Is she ever going to act like my God damn wife?*

"Maybe I'm tired of relying on people to support me. I

can earn a living. I'm smart and there's no reason I can't work for my uncle anymore."

"We agreed that once we married, you wouldn't be his paralegal."

"No, you and my uncle agreed to that." She sat on the edge of the bed. "No one gave me a say in any of this, remember?"

"We're going to get into this now?" I paced the room. "You're my wife. My responsibility. I can take care of you. End of story."

Did she think I was going to let her work for her uncle? The man who didn't value her or respect her?

"Maybe I'm tired of being someone else's responsibility. I'm tired of not knowing the world that's going on around me. I don't want to be a prisoner anymore."

"A prisoner?"

The doorbell rang before she had time to explain herself.

"Fuck," I shouted.

She got up from the bed, but I grabbed her arm before she could leave.

"We're not done," I said.

"They're here."

"They can wait. Why would you say you're a prisoner? I fucking gave you a credit card, so you'd have some freedom."

"We can talk about this later." She squeezed my hand. "Thank you for the credit card. It's difficult for me to get used to all of this."

"All of what?"

"Living here. Being your wife. Figuring out who I am."

The doorbell rang again.

"This conversation isn't over." I took her hand and led

her down the stairs. "You've completely blindsided me. I thought we were doing okay."

"We are."

"You're a difficult woman to understand." I wasn't used to getting to know the women I slept with. I was a one-night stand kind of guy before I'd married her. That lifestyle was so much easier.

When we reached the foyer, she turned and straightened my tie. It was a sweet gesture, but I wasn't sure what she was thinking, and that bothered me.

"Are you worried I won't meet your family's approval?" I moved toward the door. "I don't care what they think about me."

"We should get the door." She stepped away from me and answered it. "Hello."

Antonio, Kristina, and Alessandro stood on my porch with a bottle of wine and a huge cookie tray. They were all dressed in expensive clothes with their well-manicured hair and designer shoes. They always looked the part of an important family. I loathed these people. How did I end up in bed with them?

When I glanced at Luciana, I found my answer. It was more than her beauty that drew me in. Upon our initial introduction, I thought her innocence and naivety were an act. How could someone who grew up among the Torrios be so skittish and unsure? She must have been mistreated and cast aside her whole life. I wanted to know why they were so cruel to her.

I learned that she had edge, especially when she tried to stand up to me. Her little shots were adorable, but I sensed she wanted more with me even if she was afraid to admit it. I couldn't blame her for not wanting to let her guard down with me. I wasn't a simple man to deal with. I only trusted a small few.

Maybe it was time to let my wife in.

As I watched her embrace Sandro, I realized he had been her friend and protector. But he was the youngest male and didn't command the most respect in their family. From the outside, it had appeared that Luciana had lived a privileged life, but I had a feeling that was all smoke and mirrors. Why else would she make the comment about being my prisoner? Did she view this marriage as leaving one cell for another?

Her uncle gave her a quick hug, and she looked uncomfortable with it. Her aunt was too busy scrutinizing my home to notice Luciana.

"Romero." Antonio handed me the bottle of wine that probably cost more than it was worth. "Thank you for having us."

"Thanks for coming." I reached for Luciana's hand and brought her to my side.

Sandro gave me a disapproving look, which only made me hold her tighter.

*She belongs to me, kid.*

"What an adorable home you have here." Kristina shoved the cookie tray toward Luciana and then walked around the foyer. "Are you adjusting to such a small space?"

"It's hardly small. It's plenty big for the two of us." When Luciana smiled at me, some of my rage over Kristina's attitude subsided. "I like it here."

Did she really mean that? Because a few minutes ago she told me she was my prisoner. I couldn't keep up.

"Mom." Sandro looked down the long hall that led to the kitchen. "This house is huge."

"Not compared to ours," Kristina said. "But you are just starting out, so I guess it's appropriate."

"It's seven thousand square feet." *Why am I engaging in this?* "Would you like to join us on the patio by the pool?"

I took the cookie tray from Luciana and set it on the foyer table with the wine. I'd give them to the guards later. Luciana gave me a suspicious look, but she didn't say anything as we continued to the patio. I wouldn't give Kristina the satisfaction of serving her cookies.

Once we were situated outside, my staff served coffee and tea, and the pastries I'd ordered from my favorite Italian bakery. Kristina looked around, probably wondering where the cookies she brought were.

"Pizzelles." Luciana picked the anise cookie off the tray. "I love these."

"I know." I rested my hand on her thigh.

"How?" She broke the delicate cookie in half and set it on her plate.

"It's the only dessert you ate at our wedding." It was practically the only thing she ate because her nerves had gotten the better of her. "You seemed to enjoy it."

"She's liked them since she was a child," Antonio said. "I used to send them to her when she was at boarding school."

"Those packages were one of my few highlights while I was in school." Her body tensed when she spoke. "I always thought those deliveries were very thoughtful of you."

"Oh, please." Kristina stirred some sugar into her coffee. "It's not like your uncle thought to do it. He had his secretary take care of that. He didn't even know what was in those packages."

Anger swelled in my chest.

*I'm gonna kill this bitch.*

## CHAPTER 23

*Luciana*

Romero tightened his grip on my thigh every time my aunt spoke. Sitting between my terrifying family and my equally frightening husband had my stomach stirring and my nerves at an all-time high. How did I get thrown into the middle of this? *Oh yeah, no one offered me a choice.*

"Lu." Sandro's voice settled my anxiety. "Have you lost weight? You look so thin."

I didn't want to tell my cousin it was kind of hard trying to eat when my stomach was constantly upset. Pretending to be a dutiful wife while I betrayed my husband at every turn took a toll on me. Not to mention, I'd witnessed Romero kill two people. Eating was the last thing on my mind.

"I'm eating. I guess I'm adjusting to my new surroundings." I poured some tea into my cup. "Romero made me the most delicious French toast the other day."

"How sweet," my aunt said. "But don't you have a cook for that sort of thing?"

"We're in the process of getting one," Romero answered as he grasped my thigh even harder. If my aunt kept provoking him, my thigh would be one big bruise. "I'm looking for one who can help Luciana with her cooking skills since she was never properly taught."

"Do you expect her to clean for you too?" Sandro asked.

"Not at all," Romero said. "Learning to cook might help her adjust to her new home. Maybe it will make her feel more at ease and give her a sense of purpose."

"That's a fabulous idea." My uncle nodded. "You should learn how to cook a proper Italian Sunday meal."

"We'll see," I said. "I'm thinking about going back to school."

"You are?" Romero was taken aback by my statement, but why wouldn't he be? I'd never mentioned my plans to him before. "This is news to me."

"Not the lawyer thing again." My aunt rolled her eyes while she picked out a cookie from the tray. "We have enough of them in the family."

"What lawyer thing?" Romero turned my chair to face him in a barbaric attempt to startle me.

It worked.

"Lu wants to be a lawyer," Sandro said. "I think she'll make an awesome attorney. She's smart and pays attention to details."

"She's far too meek and mild for that," my aunt said. "We've already been over this."

"Now is not the time to discuss this." My uncle tapped the table. "We'll revisit this at a later date."

"You don't have to revisit anything with my wife." Romero pointed across the table. "If she wants to be an attorney, then she'll be an attorney."

He took my hand in his. "We'll discuss this after, but if you want to go back to school, I'll support you."

"You will?" That was a surprise. "I didn't think you'd want me to... I didn't think you'd be receptive to it."

"I might be receptive to a lot of things that involve you if you would tell me about them." He glanced at my aunt and uncle. "Luciana's decision to become an attorney doesn't concern you, especially since she no longer works for your firm."

"We can talk about it at another time." My uncle stared at me. "I already told you I would consider it and you would have a job with me when the time comes."

"You did?" My aunt tightened her lips. "Let her husband be responsible for her."

"What is your problem with Luciana?" Romero asked my aunt.

"Excuse me?" she replied. "I don't like your tone."

"I don't like the way you treat my wife," he said. "You may have gotten away with it before, but I won't allow it under my roof."

"Romero." I squeezed his hand because I didn't want a confrontation. "It's okay."

"No, it isn't." He continued to direct his wrath at my aunt.

I didn't feel sorry for her. She deserved for someone to put her in her place, and I knew Romero could do it. I didn't need any more problems. This whole situation was far too complicated as it was.

"You harbor a deep resentment for Luciana," Romero said. "I've noticed it since you offered her hand to me. You're condescending toward her, and you treat her like she's an afterthought instead of a family member."

"Romero," my uncle said, "you might want to stop this

conversation before it gets out of hand and you say something you regret. This is my wife you're speaking to."

"I rarely regret anything." Romero stood from his chair, turning his attention to the driveway. "But it appears Gio is here and we should go to my office to discuss a few business situations that concern us both."

My uncle got up from his chair.

"That's probably a good idea. I won't be long," he said to my aunt. "Have a civilized conversation with Luciana." He glanced at Sandro. "You see to it."

"As if Mom will listen to me." Sandro smirked.

"Make her," Uncle Antonio ordered.

Romero cupped the side of my face in his hand and stared at me with those fierce eyes of his before leaning down and kissing me. It wasn't just a quick peck on the lips. It had a full-blown, 'let's have sex right now' vibe. He trailed his lips along my jaw and to my ear, and I shivered from the warmth of his breath. Was it fear? Was it lust? Maybe it was a mixture of both. Whatever it was, I liked it.

"Don't let her treat you like you are beneath her," he whispered into my ear. "You're a Bilotti. Fucking act like it."

He released me from his hold, but he kept me locked in his reckless gaze until my uncle cleared his throat.

*Message received.*

As the two men walked away, my aunt stood from her chair, raised her hands in front of her, and clapped in a slow deliberate tempo. "Bravo."

"Mom?" Sandro looked at her as if she'd lost her mind. "What are you doing?"

"Congratulating, Lu." She sat back down and poured herself some more coffee. "I didn't think you had it in you, but somehow you got that barbaric man to fall for you."

"What?"

She had that all wrong.

"He's protective of you. He's comfortable referring to you as his wife and he touches and kisses you around others. The way you interact with him, well, if I didn't know any better, I'd think you were a real married couple."

"We are." Wasn't that what the ceremony and reception were for? "We live together as husband and wife. Isn't that what you wanted?"

"How is that going?" Sandro asked. "Do you like being here?"

"I don't know." Maybe I would if I wasn't lying to Romero all the time. "It hasn't been that long."

"Do you sleep in the same bed?" He cringed. "That's got to be strange."

"Of course they do," my aunt said. "How else do you think she got him to fall for her so quickly? I'm impressed. I mean, most women would have figured out that using her body and her charms were the best ways to get what she wanted from someone like Romero, but I didn't think you would go that far. Neither did your husband, which is why he trusts you so easily."

"He doesn't trust me." I shook my head because if Romero knew the things I had found in his office and leaked to my family... "He's guarded and careful. He doesn't make mistakes."

"Not yet, but he will." Aunt Kristina was so sure of herself. "You keep doing what you're doing and we'll have everything we need from him."

"What exactly is that?" I asked.

"You don't have to worry about that," she said. "Leave it to your uncle."

It was obvious my family's plan was not about seeing if Romero was a worthy business associate. It never was. They wanted to take what he had. What he had worked so hard for.

Should it matter to me? Everything Romero gained was through illegal means. If I could, I would walk away from all of this in a heartbeat.

Maybe not all of it.

*You're a Bilotti.* Why did those words mean so much to me? Because for the first time in my life, I felt like I belonged. It wasn't a perfect situation, but Romero wanted me here. He wanted me to be his wife. I had a place by his side, but I had no right to claim that spot. Not after what I had done to him. What they still expected me to do to him.

"We have little time," my aunt said. "I need any details about Romero's day-to-day operations, as you can recall. I'd also like a rundown of his schedule."

"His schedule?" I asked.

"His comings and goings," Sandro clarified. "Who visits and who he lets into his circle."

I stood from my chair and walked around the patio, glancing inside the house to make sure Romero wasn't nearby. "When I agreed to help you with this matter, it was to see if you could trust him as an associate. As far as I can tell, he has done nothing to betray you. As a matter of fact, he seems to take all of your business suggestions and has used your recommendations when it comes to his purchases."

"Are you running his territory?" My aunt lit a cigarette. "You're not here to question one fucking thing we're doing. Do you understand?"

I looked to Sandro for help, but he focused on the ground, avoiding eye contact with me. As much as I loved him, he would never go against his mother for me. I would never ask him to.

"Lu?" My aunt raised her voice. "Are we clear?"

"I think if you looked closely at the situation, you would see that Romero would make a formidable ally. He's young, strong, and smart. He can only further your agenda."

"It appears as if Romero isn't the only one who believes this is a real marriage." She cackled as she tapped her long nails on the table. "Whatever the two of you do in his bed isn't my concern, but you have a job to complete. I suggest you do it if you want a family to come home to when all of this is over."

"I'm doing the best I can do. I risk my life every time I spy on him and report back to the Torrios." What else did they want from me?

"Lu." Sandro placed his hand on my shoulder. "Answer the questions and this will all be over real soon."

*What if I don't want it to be over?*

∽

A FEW HOURS LATER, I quietly made my way downstairs to get a glass of water. I hadn't seen Romero since my family left. They had put him in a foul mood, so I thought it was best for me to retreat to the bedroom.

His mood wasn't the only reason I went into hiding, though. I had an overwhelming sense of guilt after giving my aunt and cousin such detailed information about my husband's schedule. If I thought I was in deep before…

"Luciana," Romero's deep voice called to me from his study as I walked into the hallway.

I froze when the sound of his footsteps came toward the ajar door. Did he know what I had done today? Had someone listened to my conversation with Aunt Kristina and Sandro? My stomach wanted to heave all those cookies

I'd eaten. I was on the verge of tears when he opened the door. What would I do if he confronted me?

"What are you doing out here in the hall?" He took my hand and guided me into the study.

"I was thirsty."

"Sit down." He pointed at the plush, black leather sofa.

"I don't want to bother you." I bit my lip as I glanced at a stack of papers on his desk. "You look busy."

"I am busy, but I want to talk to you." He sat, and then pulled me down next to him. "Are you okay?"

"Why wouldn't I be?"

"You seem jittery." He rubbed my leg. "More anxious than usual."

"I'm not."

"I can't say that I'd blame you after that terrible visit with those people." He draped his arm over my back and coaxed me closer to him. "I can't even bring myself to call them your family."

"That's who they are though." As much as I hated admitting that, it couldn't be denied. "I'm used to it."

"You don't need to take their shit," he said. "You have to learn to stand up for yourself."

"They aren't easy people to stand up to."

"People will treat you the way you let them." He clenched his fist in his lap, all his muscles coiling in response. I didn't like seeing him this tense. He could snap at any moment, and I didn't want to be on the receiving end of his anger. "I don't like the way they treat you."

"Can we change the subject?"

"You're impossible." He sighed. "If you don't stand up for yourself, I'm going to have to do it and no one will like that."

If I didn't already feel guilty about the information I'd

provided my family today, I certainly did now. Why was he being so nice to me?

"Were you serious about law school?" he asked. "Or is that something you bring up because they wouldn't let you do it?"

"I'm very serious about it."

"Why haven't you told me?"

"We don't really know one another that well." How ridiculous was that? We were married. "I guess it never came up."

"I think you should do it." He turned me to face him. "Start looking at schools tomorrow. Get yourself enrolled."

"I have to finish my degree. I only have an associate's degree. This is going to take a while."

"You've got nothing but time." He trailed his finger across my lips. "And I have nothing but money, so we're all set."

"Why would you do this for me?"

"Why wouldn't I?" He cupped the side of my face in his hand and rubbed my cheek with his thumb. "You're not my prisoner, Luciana. You belong to me, but you deserve to explore who you are."

He dipped his head and kissed me. It was softer than usual. Not the hurried, animalistic pace I'd grown accustomed to with him. He took his time, probing my mouth with his tongue, massaging it against mine as he twirled his fingers in my hair.

As he released me from his hold, I inhaled a deep breath, realizing how much I'd needed that kiss. When I gazed into his eyes, he tilted his head and stared at me, almost as if I'd stunned him.

"Thank you for the offer to go back to school." I gently kissed his cheek. "I accept."

"Good." He grabbed my upper arms. "I meant what I said earlier."

"You say a lot of things." I swallowed hard as I tried to relax under his stone-cold gaze. "What are you referring to?"

"You are a Bilotti."

*If you only knew how much of a Bilotti I've become.*

## CHAPTER 24

*Romero*

"Why do the shipments always come in the middle of the night?" Gio asked as we inspected the latest cargo that had been delivered to the warehouse.

"Why do you think?" I checked the final box of merchandise. "Fuck!"

"What?"

"Another box of shit." I launched it across the room. "None of this merchandise is worth what we paid. I doubt any of it even works."

"You should have killed the remaining two that day in the woods."

"I didn't think they'd be stupid enough to double cross me." I took out my phone and sent a cryptic message to my top two enforcers who were waiting outside the hideaway where the two assholes who sold me these shit guns lived. My men would know what I expected of them. "Now I have to recoup my money and finish the job I started in the woods."

"Johnny and Frankie will handle it."

"They better." I tossed my phone on my desk. "Have them contact me when it's done."

"I don't think the sellers were smart enough to pull this off on their own."

"You don't think I already suspect that?" I didn't want to believe it, but I couldn't shake the feeling that my alliance with the Torrios was a setup. "None of this makes sense. They sought me out and wanted to join the two families. I only moved as quickly as I did because Giancarlo advised me to."

"Too many little things aren't sitting well with me."

"Like what?"

"Well, Arturo's disappearance and this shit product are two big red flags, but there has been other stuff that has put me on edge."

"What kind of stuff and why is this the first I'm hearing of it?" I trusted Gio to handle my affairs, but he needed to keep me in the loop.

"I'm in the process of confirming a few things but word on the street is people know intimate details about our business that they shouldn't."

"The club negotiations?" I was in the process of expanding my legitimate business to keep the Feds off my back. I often bought bars, clubs and restaurants that were in need of financial assistance. I kept the ones that turned a profit and the ones that didn't, I sold to bigger corporations who wanted the properties.

"At first it wasn't anything that concerned me but when guys knew we were negotiating properties in the city, well, that caught my attention. We're good at keeping things quiet until we're ready to sell what we don't want."

"Only a select few know about the clubs."

That was by design. If real estate moguls knew what I

was after, they would swoop in and undercut me. I had to have the upper hand so I could sell for a huge profit when the property was in high demand.

"I'm trying to narrow it down and figure out where the leak is coming from."

"You think we have a mole inside the organization?" We were so careful. I kept my circle small for a reason.

"I don't know." Gio looked down at the cement ground.

"What aren't you telling me?"

"Let me do my job and confirm a few things before I bring you what I have."

"What the fuck does that mean? Tell me what you have and we'll take care of it."

"I don't have anything solid, but I will in a day or two. These things take time. Let me handle this. It's my job, remember?"

"If Torrio set us up, I'll burn his fucking house down with them all in it." I slammed my fist against the wall. "I should have fucking known! It's bad enough the way they treat my wife, but I'll kill them if I find out they're coming after us."

"They are Lu's family."

"I'm Luciana's family." If this was a double cross at least I got her away from them. "They made sure of that."

"Yeah, I guess they did." Gio clenched his fist by his side. "That arranged marriage never seemed right to me."

"They don't give a shit about my wife. Her aunt couldn't wait to hand her over to me." The more I thought about the callous way Kristina handled the marriage negotiations, the more enraged I became. I didn't know Luciana then, so when Kristina said the things she did, they didn't mean much to me.

"My niece is a bit of a problem child," she had said. "She

needs a special type of man to deal with her. Someone who will put her in her place and make her understand the world we live in."

That horrible woman was giving me permission to hurt Luciana. And I fell for it. The night of our engagement party, I ripped that dress right off her without caring about her feelings. I thought she was testing me, like she was some entitled mafia brat who needed my structure. That was what her aunt wanted me to believe.

"Luciana is better off with me."

"I hope you're right."

"What the fuck, Gio?" I grabbed him by his shirt. "Why would you say that? I'm not Dad. I'm not going to hurt her the way he hurt our mother."

"That's not what I meant." He shoved me off him. "I know you wouldn't hurt her on purpose, but if she pushed you too far…Look, I never liked this alliance idea. I didn't think joining the two families was particularly beneficial to us but we're in it now. So, let me figure out what's going on and I'll bring you whatever I have as soon as I know it's reliable."

"I'd much rather you tell me right now."

When his phone rang, he pulled it from his pocket and glanced at the screen. "I need to take this." He pointed to the door. "I'll be outside."

"Gio," I called after him. "I'm sorry I overreacted a few minutes ago."

"We're cool." He stepped outside and answered his call.

I sat on the edge of the crappy, metal desk in the warehouse and tried to calm down. The useless shipment put me in a bad mood. Finding out that I had a possible breach in my organization didn't help matters. None of this made sense. What did the Torrios want with me? They already had my father's territory. They weren't interested in my particular business dealings, so why did they seek me out?

I paced the damp warehouse, trying to answer all the rapid questions cluttering inside my head. Questions I should have had the answers to long before I entered into such a hasty alliance. I only had myself to blame, but what was done was done.

If anything right came out of this, it was Luciana. We didn't have the perfect marriage, but we were getting there. She still wasn't as comfortable around me as I would like, and I could admit most of that was my fault. I was trying. Maybe I needed to try harder.

If a war began between the Torrios and the Bilottis, Luciana would be caught in the middle. Would she choose them or us? I hadn't given her much reason to choose me, but neither had her family. I needed to make her see I was the better option. I'd give her the life she deserved. She had to give me the chance to prove I could be the man she needed.

It was nearly four in the morning, but I had the urge to call her and tell her I was working and I would be home soon. She was probably sleeping. A text would be better. At least she would see it if she woke up and know I was thinking about her.

As I was about to compose the text, Gio came back inside. He closed the door behind him.

"Was the call important?" I asked.

"We have a problem."

"Tell me." I shoved my phone back in my pocket. My text to my wife would have to wait. "What's the problem?"

"They found Arturo."

"And?"

"He was beaten and tortured and left to die in a field behind one of our safe houses."

"What the fuck! How did they even find the safe house?"

"We don't know yet, but they left the money with him."

"They're sending me a message." I flipped the desk over and kicked the side of it. "He had a daughter and, oh God, his mother. I need to take care of them."

"We'll set up a trust for his daughter, and his mother will be taken care of." He held up his phone so I could see the pictures our guys sent of the scene. "I don't think we can send him home to his mother. She can't have an open casket."

"Fuck." I pushed his hand away. "She's going to want a body. She's Catholic. Call Charlie and have him retrieve the body. Have them put Arturo in another location and then call it in."

I rubbed my temples. "Once the morgue has him, have our undertaker handle it. Maybe he can work some magic so his mother can say goodbye."

"That's going to be a lot of magic." Gio looked at the photos. "We need to find the scum that did this."

"We will but first, we need to figure out who the spy is." I hated to think one of my men could betray me like this. "Go through cell records, look at the footage at the house and where the guys stay. I want this dealt with swiftly and painfully. I don't care how much it costs and I don't care what means our team has to go through to get this information."

"I told you I'm already on it."

"Gio, find out who betrayed me."

"I will."

"I have a message of my own to send." The damaged merchandise in the corner of the room infuriated me.

"When I find out who did this, I'm coming for them, and I'm coming at them with everything I have. I'll leave no one standing."

"Let me get it all figured out," Gio said. "I promise I'll sort it out."

"No fucking survivors."

∞

I TOOK my time heading home because I needed to calm down before I climbed into bed with my wife. She was the only thing right in my world. Who would have thought that? For years, the only person I could depend on was my brother, but that was changing. I was slowly coming around and realizing I needed Luciana too.

Maybe she could make me forget my tortured childhood and help me come to terms with the things I'd done, and the man I had become. Together, we could heal one another. Once she accepted I wanted to be her husband in every sense of the word, maybe she would begin to trust me and what we could build together.

We started this relationship off from the wrong place. That was her family's fault. They should have given us time to get to know one another. I should have demanded that but instead, I did something uncharacteristic. I moved with haste. I jumped into this arrangement because if everything went according to plan, my business would grow and I would gain more power and respect in the organized crime world. But, if I was totally honest with myself, I was far too intrigued by who the Torrios were offering me.

When I saw Luciana at the bar at that wedding, I wanted her. I didn't understand how much that desire to covet her was until Antonio dangled her in front of me. Now that I had her, I would do everything in my power to keep her. Of course, that might prove to be a problem if it turned out her family was the one betraying me. I'd have to eliminate them and figure out a way to keep my wife by my side.

When I came through the front door, glass shattered against the wall, narrowly missing my head. I reached for my gun and spun around, catching a glimpse of my furious wife dressed in a short pink silk robe standing on the staircase with another crystal vase she had poached from the table on the upstairs landing.

She glared at me before launching the vase in my direction. I stepped out of the way and let it crash to the floor of the foyer, shattering into thousands of pieces.

My cock hardened at the sight of her filled with rage. The robe had come undone, revealing her silver thong and bare breasts. She looked so fucking hot. Just the distraction I needed after this clusterfuck of a night.

"Oh, baby." I smirked as I set my gun on the foyer table. "You have no idea how much I need this fight today."

**CHAPTER 25**

*Luciana*

I hurried down the steps, ready to advance my smug husband, but he stopped me before I could step onto the hardwood covered in shattered glass.

"You'll cut your feet."

"Like you care."

"What's got you so upset, butterfly?"

"Don't call me that!" I shoved at his chest. "Where were you?"

"Working."

"At five in the morning?" I placed my hand on my hip. "You're lying."

"Why would I lie about working?" He unbuttoned his shirt and tugged it out of his pants.

"Who are you fucking?" I tried to hold back the tears, but the thought of him being with another woman enraged me.

"What?"

"Do you think I'm stupid?"

My uncle had so many women on the side through the years. He often didn't come home until early in the morning. My cousins were constantly stringing women along. Desperate women who would do anything to be with a rich, dangerous, and powerful man.

How many women would kill to be by my husband's side?

"I've been at the warehouse all night wasting my time with a phony shipment."

"All night?"

"Yes, you can ask Gio if you don't believe me."

"Like Gio wouldn't lie for you?" I yelled as I opened and closed my fists at my sides. No one had ever evoked this kind of fury from me before. "I don't believe you."

"Have I ever given you any reason not to believe me?" He grabbed my throat and shoved my back into the wall, pressing his body against mine. "You need to calm the fuck down. I don't like your insinuation, and I don't answer to you."

"Let go of me." I struggled out of his hold, but he tightened his grip on my throat and pushed his erection against my stomach. "Haven't you figured out I like when you fight me? I'm so hard for you right now."

"You're disgusting."

"If I'm so disgusting, why do you care if I'm fucking someone else?" When he leaned into my face, I turned my head. "Don't move away from me."

With his fingers still pressed against my throat, he moved my chin with his thumb and attacked my mouth with his lips, but I was too angry to give in. I didn't know what came over me but with one swift action, I bit his lip, stopping when I tasted the coppery liquid in my mouth.

"Ouch!" He pushed me back and wiped his mouth, looking down at the smeared blood on the back of his hand. "You little bitch."

He came at me so fast, I couldn't get out of the way. He slammed his body against mine, pinning me against the wall.

"Stop it!" I screamed.

"You started this." He gazed down at my open robe and my bare breasts. "But I'm going to finish it."

He grabbed my breast and squeezed it. "I've had a long night and I don't expect to come home to this disrespect in my house."

"Get off me." I clawed at his shirt, pushing it down his shoulder as I tried to struggle out of his hold. "We're not doing this."

"The fuck we aren't."

When I hit his chest, he gripped my wrists in his hands. His hold was tight, but only hard enough to subdue me. He fought me enough to keep me away from him but didn't hurt me. The more I wiggled, the tighter he held me. It was no use; he was too strong for me.

"What has gotten into you?" He kissed my lips before pressing his forehead to mine and releasing my hands. "Why are you so angry with me?"

"You always talk about how I belong to you and how I'm yours."

"You are."

"You belong to me too."

Why was I admitting any of this to him? I wasn't supposed to care about him. Why did it bother me if he'd found a side whore to spend his nights with? The idea of me being upset was all too absurd. I was betraying him far more than him screwing around could ever betray me. But as I stared into his gorgeous eyes and remembered all the ways he tried to be my husband, I couldn't help myself. I wanted him to be mine.

"I'm not going to allow you to screw whoever you want and then expect me to be here with my legs open and waiting for you."

"I'm not allowed?"

When he laughed, something inside me snapped.

"You don't get to tell me what I'm allowed to do," he said. "I don't answer to anyone. And, you will open your legs for me whenever I tell you to."

He continued to laugh at me, making me feel as worthless and as useless as I'd felt my entire life. I wasn't having it anymore. I was tired of being alone and undervalued as a person.

"Get away from me!" I swung my arms in an attempt to push him away. When my hand hit his cheek, the sting rattled my core. If it hurt me that much, I knew he felt it.

"Romero, I'm... I didn't mean to." I inched away from him, but he caught me by my arms and threw me down onto the steps. He dropped down on top of me and with a recklessly wild glint in his eyes.

"Luciana, I will not let you turn me into my father." He reached between us and ripped my thong off in one quick motion. "You have no idea how much I'm going to enjoy this."

"No." I thrashed and kicked, fighting him off me.

"Keep fighting me, baby. That will only make me fuck you harder."

"I don't want to." I managed to turn in his arms and escape his hold. When he reached for me, he grabbed my robe, pulling it from me as I hurried up the steps. As I ran down the hall, his footsteps gained on me. My heart raced inside my chest as I got closer to the bedroom.

"Keep running." He laughed as he grabbed my hair and took me down, forcing me onto my stomach on the hardwood floor outside the bedroom. "I'm going to make you regret all of that fire inside you."

As he held me still with one hand, he undid his belt and tugged it through the loops. When I looked over my shoulder, I screamed out in fear as he wrapped the leather around his hand.

"I'd hold still if I were you." When he raised his hand, I turned my face and steadied myself on all fours. "You need to settle down and remember I'm in control."

"Romero!" I cried out when the leather slapped across my backside. "No!"

When he hit me again, I yelled louder, but then I realized it didn't hurt as much as I thought it would. *Why is he holding back?* He ran the leather across my cheeks and between my legs, rubbing it against my clit.

I jumped when he gripped my hip and slid the belt between my legs. He pushed on my back, raising my backside in the air, so he could hit me again. This time it was harder, but I was too distracted when he shoved his fingers inside my wet sex to worry about the hot sting of the belt against my tender skin. In a strange way, it was arousing.

I arched my back and rocked my hips in time with his fingers. The cold wood floor chilled my heated skin.

"Please." I didn't know if I was begging him to stop hitting me or if I was asking for more. My nipples ached for his attention and my body twitched as he brought me closer to climax.

"Do you like my belt?" He assaulted my flesh a few more times with violent whacks before abandoning the strap and lowering his lips to my shoulder. "I haven't paid this ass much attention."

He flattened his tongue along my skin, licking and kissing where he had hit me. "How far will you let me take this?"

"I don't..." I closed my eyes and scratched at the floor when he spread my cheeks open and swirled his tongue around the rim of my ass. "Oh..."

This was the filthiest thing he'd ever done to me, but it felt so good.

He slithered his hands around my waist and to my pussy, pushing his fingers inside me. He moved them in and out of me as he continued to lick me.

"You're soaked. I'll have to take my belt to your ass more often."

I pushed my hips back, rocking against his hand, aching for more. My stomach coiled as I clenched around his fingers.

"Tell me what you want." He withdrew his fingers and slapped my backside.

"Ouch!"

"Tell me."

"I want you."

"Where do you want me? Here?" He pressed the tip of his cock against my hot, wet sex. "Inside you?"

"Yes," I moaned.

"Who do you belong to?" He shifted his pelvis, giving me a little bit more.

"You." I wiggled against him, but he grabbed my hips and held me still.

"Who's in control?"

"Please." I couldn't take it anymore.

"Answer my question or I'll stop and make you take my cock in your mouth and you'll never get any relief."

The pressure building between my legs caused me to tremble all over. Sweat trickled down my back and the air in my lungs came out in erratic breaths.

"Who is in control?" His voice vibrated through me.

"You are."

"Apologize for disrespecting me and giving me shit after I had a long, hard day at work." He slammed his waist forward, but only gave me a little more of his swollen erection. "If you do that, you can have all of me."

"I'm sorry!" I screamed out. "Please fuck me."

"It would be my pleasure." He sheathed himself completely in my hot juices. "I own your pussy."

"Yes."

After two forceful thrusts, I unraveled into a long, hard orgasm. My head spun as my heart strummed loudly between my ears. The force of my climax left me lightheaded and too weak to even move with him, so I let him pound into me as I tingled with the aftershocks of my release.

He lifted me up so that my back smacked against his broad chest.

"Are you still with me? You came so fast." He kissed my neck and cupped my breasts in his hand. "I thought you might have passed out."

I leaned my head back and stretched my neck, seeking out his lips. "Kiss me."

He trailed his hand along my neck and guided my chin up until our lips met. He dominated the connection by forcing his tongue into my mouth and massaging it along mine. As we kissed, he kept what seemed like a never-ending pace inside me.

"Luciana." He jostled me forward, forcing me to the floor. "I'm going to come."

He twisted his pelvis and held onto my hips as he emptied inside me, claiming me once again as his. After he caught his breath, he stood from the floor, and then scooped me up and carried me to the bed. He placed me in the center before pulling the comforter back and pointing for me to get under.

He undressed, removing what was left of his clothes, shoes, and socks. I couldn't take my gaze away from his beautifully sculpted body. After he dropped his watch and phone on the dresser beside the bed, he climbed in and joined me under the covers.

He wrapped his arms around me and guided me onto his chest, surrounding me in his warmth and protection. Why were we so volatile with one another? Why couldn't we be a normal couple?

*You know why.*

"I'm sorry I hit you." I ran my fingers along his cheek. "It was an accident. I was mad, but I would never do that on purpose."

"I know."

"When you didn't come home, I thought the worst."

He stroked my hair. "I'm not cheating on you, Luciana. When I said our vows, I meant them." He took my hand and raised it between our faces. "When I put these rings on your finger that meant something to me too."

"Romero." The tears streamed down my cheeks before I could stop them.

"Why are you crying?" He kissed my face, trying to soothe me, which only made me feel worse. "I told you I'm not cheating on you. I don't want anyone but you."

"I know, it's that I..." *Pull it together. He'll kill you if he knows what you did.* "I don't deserve you."

"Don't say that." His facial features twisted into a terrifying display of anger. "That's your family making you talk like that. They made you think you weren't worthy of so much, but it's not true. They did you wrong, but I intend to fix all of that."

"I don't need you to fix it."

"I want to."

"When we were downstairs you said you wouldn't let me turn you into your father."

"Did I?"

"What did you mean?"

"I don't want to talk about it." He pulled me into his side and kissed the top of my head. "I need to get some sleep. I have to be up in a few hours."

"You said you'd let me get to know you better. When is that going to happen?"

"You know me better than most people." He twirled his finger in my hair. "Can't that be enough?"

"I don't feel like I know you at all."

Silence fell over the room as the sun began to filter in from behind the blinds. I closed my eyes and tried to clear my mind. I was in too deep. My family expected me to keep spying on my husband. When I took on this assignment, it was supposed to help them determine if they could trust Romero. As far as I could tell, they could. If they would have kept their word, I might have had a chance with Romero. But now, I couldn't see a future with him. No matter how much I wanted one.

"My father used to beat my mother," he said.

"I'm sorry." I thought he had fallen asleep. I didn't expect him to continue the conversation, but he must have been trying to find the right way to express his thoughts.

"The belt... that wasn't about anger or trying to hurt you." His body tensed against mine. "I know I'm rough and I manhandle you and I'm not always gentle, but I won't strike you in anger. I learned a lot of bad habits from my father, and I don't always treat you the way I should, but I can control my impulses. Most of the time."

"You do scare me most of the time, but I'm trying to believe you won't hurt me."

"I want to believe I would never hurt you either. I'm cruel and ruthless, but I'm trying to tone it down when it comes to you."

"You grew up in an abusive home. I can't imagine what it must have been like for you to know your mom was being abused."

"I don't like to talk about my mother. It triggers memories that I've buried deep inside. Memories that I don't need to recall. My soul is dark enough."

"I don't think your soul is dark." I curled up closer to him. "I think you've chosen a life that makes you believe you're a dark person."

"This life chose me."

"What would happen if we ran away from all of it?"

"Are you being funny?"

"No," I whispered. "What if we walked away?"

If I could get him to agree to run away with me, we could be free of all the violence, the secrets, and the betrayal. Maybe I had it all wrong. I always thought when I ran away from my family, I'd be escaping alone, but what if I was meant to be with Romero?

"My sweet, naive, Luciana." He held me close to him, making me feel warm and protected. "There's no running for me. I've made choices that will keep me in this business until I'm six feet under."

"I don't think you want to be here anymore than I do."

"It's not so bad with you here." He shrugged. "You let me take care of the business and keeping you safe. You concentrate on figuring out a plan for school. That's what I want you to do."

"I'd much rather run away with you."

"Maybe someday."

## CHAPTER 26

*Romero*

When I got out of the shower and came into the bedroom, Luciana was leaning over the dresser putting on her lipstick.

"Wow." I looked her over, admiring her sexy ass in the tight black skirt she wore. "I might have to come over there and fuck you."

Her luscious lips curved into a delectable smile. "We can do that later."

Her hair was blown out straight and sleek, and her makeup was a little heavier than when she hung around the house. She paired the black skirt with a gray, shimmery buttoned down dress shirt and black stilettos.

"You're telling me no?"

"I'm telling you we can do whatever you want later."

"That sounds promising." I dried my hair with my towel before going into my closet. "Where are you headed?"

"To the city."

*The city?*

"I'm going to the firm."

"Why?" I leaned against the doorframe of the closet not liking her plans at all. "What do you have to do there?"

"I haven't been there in a while." She placed her lipstick in her pocketbook. "I never got a chance to get my stuff from my desk."

"I'll send someone to do that for you."

"I want to do it."

"Why?"

"I want to." She came toward me and took my hands in hers. "Closure."

"What are you saying?"

"I don't want to be under my family's thumb anymore. I feel like I need to go to the firm one last time."

"Do you want me to come with you?"

This was the best news she could have given me. If she walked away from her family, whatever Gio had for me today about the Torrios would make breaking this alliance much easier.

"I can do this by myself."

"What exactly is it that you'll be doing?"

"I want to tell my cousins I'm going back to school and you're supporting my decision to become a lawyer. I want them to know I'm becoming my own person. That I'm finally getting to do something I've wanted to do for a long time. Does that make sense?"

"I don't want them to hurt you."

She didn't need to tell them anything. The further she separated herself from them the better.

"They won't." She kissed my cheek and let go of my hands. "I'm a Bilotti, remember?"

"Don't you forget it."

"I'll be back this afternoon."

"You have Jag drive you right to the door and you text him when you're ready to leave." I reached for her hand. "I don't want you alone in the city."

Now that she was my wife, she was on people's radar. I didn't need any of my enemies coming for her, especially since I didn't know who had targeted Arturo.

"Okay."

"Do you want to go see a movie tonight?"

"Like at the theater?" She smiled. "With popcorn?"

"I heard you like butter on your popcorn."

"I do." She laughed. "I'd love to."

"Then it's a date." If I had known taking her to see a movie would make her face light up like that, I'd have bought a God damn movie theater for her. I still might.

"Our first one."

"That's my fault." I took her face between my hands. "I promise I'll be a better husband."

"I want to be a better wife."

"You're the best wife I could have asked for. I'm not an easy man to deal with." When I kissed her, the taste of her strawberry lip gloss lingered on my lips. "I want this to be a real marriage."

"I do too."

"Don't be too long. I like when you're in the house. It calms me."

"I'll be back soon." She stayed close to me. "Romero."

"What is it?" The conflict in her eyes bothered me. She wanted to tell me something. "What's wrong?"

"Nothing." When she kissed me softly, the tenderness in her touch threw me off balance. For the first time in my life, I wanted more. How unexpected. "Everything finally seems right."

"What took you so long?" I asked as Gio came into my study with a stack of files.

"It's raining and traffic is a nightmare."

"Did you get what I wanted?"

"Yeah." He sat down and set the files next to him. "So, I've been working on this for a few days. I wanted to make sure I was absolutely sure before I brought you anything. Had our best guys working on it. Accessing emails, text messages, and locations. I cross referenced when I could and used other investigations to back up my findings."

"What did you find?" I didn't like the way he was presenting this to me. "Give it to me straight."

"There isn't going to be an easy way to tell you any of this."

"Is it the Torrios?"

"Yes."

"I fucking knew it!" I pounded my fist on my desk. "I know they were double-crossing me. Did they take out Arturo?"

"I can't confirm that yet, but they definitely dumped his body at the safe house. He disappeared before you agreed to the alliance, so I don't know if they had him this whole time or if they were working with someone else."

"What can you confirm?" I pointed at the files. "What do they say about that scumbag family?"

"There's detailed phone records here. There's a lot of texts that are cryptic but if you read between the lines, you get the gist. The call logs support times and dates when things had gone wrong for us, and they were relayed to the Torrios."

"Who is the rat?" I stood and held out my hand for the

files. "I want to know because I'm the one who will take them out."

"I don't know how to tell you this, but you might want to sit back down."

"Why?"

"What I'm about to tell you is hard. That's why I came with the proof that couldn't be disputed. I knew you'd need that but, it's not going to make any of this easier."

"Gio? Get to the fucking point. What could be worse than the family that I formed an alliance with, fucking married into, are the ones who are trying to bring me down? When did I ever ask for easy?"

"When I say the Torrios betrayed you, I mean they *all* betrayed you."

"I wouldn't expect anything less." I sat back down. "I'm glad I got Luciana away from them. She'll grieve for them, but she'll understand I did what I had to do to protect her."

"You're not understanding me."

"What am I missing? Fucking say it."

"Luciana is the traitor."

"Don't even play around like that. What's a matter with you? You joke at a time like this?" There was something amiss in my brother's expression, but I didn't want to see it. "Tell me what you know."

"I wish I was joking, but how do you think they got all the information on us?" He closed his eyes and shook his head. "I have the proof."

"Your proof is wrong." I refused to listen to what he was saying. "They set her up too."

"I considered that, but that's not what happened." He opened the folder and slid it in front of me. "It's all here, but I can give you the short version. All of our breaches happened right after you married her."

I looked down at the report in front of me, picking up a few words here and there but I was too angry to comprehend what I read. "What do I need to know?"

"According to her phone records, she's been reporting back to her family on a daily basis. Mostly, Vincent and her uncle. She's not as careful in her texts to Sandro. In those messages our guy was able to figure out what she has been feeding her family."

"You're sure?"

A blinding rage rushed over me. There was no build-up, no benefit of the doubt. Just a quick sprint to accept what I knew my brother had uncovered. This alliance never made any sense to me.

"Why didn't I follow my gut?" I threw the folder across the room. "I knew I couldn't trust that despicable family."

"We can salvage what they've done."

"Can you bring Arturo back?"

"I wish I could," he said.

"Luciana told them where the safe house was located." I slammed my fist against the desk. "She's been spying on me and going through my stuff for weeks. How did I let that happen?"

"You trusted her."

"That's a mistake I'll never make again."

"What do you want to do about her?"

"Same thing I'd do to any other traitor." I glanced at our wedding photo on my desk. That day had never meant anything to her. "I'll make her pay."

"There's something else you should see." He handed me another folder. "Our guy uncovered it when he was digging into Luciana's past."

I opened the file and studied the photos from a horrific

car accident before reading a detailed autopsy report on the two people inside the car.

"That autopsy report was buried deep. It's not the one that was released when her parents died."

"The car crash didn't kill them?"

"I'd say it was the bullet they both took to the back of their head that did it, but I'm no expert." He shrugged. "I thought this might be something we could use as leverage."

"This is a matter for another day." I tossed the file on my desk. "Thanks for getting all of this for me."

"I wish it wasn't what it is." Gio gripped the back of the sofa. "I know you have feelings for her. Maybe you could talk to her and listen to what she has to say."

"Are you fucking kidding me?"

"All I'm saying is, she isn't cunning enough for this. If you read the texts between her and Sandro, you'll see what I mean."

"I don't care what she has to say. She betrayed me. That's something I'm not going to forgive."

"Where is she?"

"In the city." I threw my hand in the air. "Visiting her cousins. How appropriate."

"Why don't you let me intercept her and put her up in a hotel tonight? I'll guard her myself. It will give you time to cool off and think more rationally."

"Nice try, Gio, but I'll be handling my wife."

"I don't think that's a good idea."

"Why? Do you think I'm going to do what Dad did to Mom?" I laughed but not because it was funny. "In that case, Mom didn't deserve the shit she took from him. Luciana is not innocent."

"What are you saying? Your wife deserves to die for this?"

"I'm saying she deserves whatever I do to her." When I stood, I knocked my chair over. "She came into my house and pretended to be my wife. She slept next to me. Hell, she even let me take her virginity. That shows you how invested she was in helping her family. She let them trade her innocence to take me down. I bought all of it."

"Maybe it wasn't an act." He pointed at me. "Think about it. You're too fucking smart to be played, especially by a girl who is afraid of her own shadow. Some of it had to be real."

"You know what, I need to be alone right now."

"I don't think you should be alone when Lu gets home."

"What is wrong with you? She needs to pay for what she's done to us, to this family." *To me.*

"I'm trying to protect you."

"You don't have to protect me, little brother. I've taken care of far worse than this."

"It's not your ability to take care of the situation I'm worried about." He stepped toward my desk, the concern in his eyes rattled me. "It's how you'll deal with the way you handle this particular problem after you do it that bothers me."

"I appreciate your concern, but it's not necessary." I motioned toward the door. "I'm sure you have things to take care of today. If you could be the point person for Arturo's final arrangements that would really help."

"I can do that from here," he said. "I don't have to leave you."

"I want to be alone." I had a lot to process, and I didn't need my brother hovering over me. "Go take care of things for me. That's what I need you to do today."

"Fine, I'll do what you ask, but I want you to think long and hard before you act on this problem." He headed for the door. "I'll check in on you later."

What he meant was he would check on what I had done to deal with Luciana. I had several ideas, but none of them would completely satisfy me. I was going to have to get creative when it came to my wife.

Revenge didn't always come swiftly.

# CHAPTER 27

*Luciana*

I took a calming breath as I walked down the hall of the firm I'd gone to every day before marrying Romero. It seemed different now, less intimidating. Knowing that I didn't have to spend every minute of every hour trying to please my uncle, Vincent, and Rocco took a lot of the anxiety away from being in this building.

Of course, now I had a whole new set of worries.

I wasn't sure why I'd even come here today, but when I woke up this morning, I decided I wanted a change. I couldn't be caught between two families anymore. I had done what my uncle asked of me, but in the process, I found that my loyalties were with my husband. Or at least, that was the way I wanted it.

How was I going to make my family see that I couldn't keep up this scam any longer? I'd fallen for the mark. I was probably the worst spy in history.

"Lu." Rocco came out of his office and motioned for me to go inside. "What are you doing here?"

I entered without answering because I didn't know what I was there for.

"Is everything okay?" He shut the door. "Are you in trouble?"

*If falling in love with the man I'm supposed to be betraying is trouble then, yes, I guess I'm in trouble.* "No."

"Do you have information because if you do, that's probably something you'll want to discuss with my dad or Vincent."

"I don't have anything new." I sat in the chair across from his desk and set my hands in my lap, trying to keep them still. "I need advice."

"About?"

"This whole situation."

He sat on the edge of his desk, crossing his legs at his ankles. "What about it? From what I hear, you're doing a fantastic job. You should be proud of yourself."

"For what?"

"Finding your place in this family. You've always said you didn't fit in, but the first time we asked you for something you stepped up and delivered."

"Because I didn't know what I was getting into."

"What do you mean?"

"I didn't realize how difficult it would be to be two people."

"Lu, what are you talking about?" He sat in the chair next to me. "Are you sure you're okay?"

"I don't know how much longer I can do this. I'm scared all the time. I'm afraid I'll get caught. I'm anxious Romero will figure out what I'm doing." I tried to hold back the tears. "I'm constantly sick to my stomach. I don't eat. I barely sleep and when I do, I dream that I'm going to get caught."

"Is that bastard hurting you?" He clenched his fist. "What has he done?"

"No, you don't understand."

"Make me understand."

"Rocco, I'm being torn in half." How could I explain that I couldn't separate my feelings? How could anyone expect me to give myself to a man in the most intimate of ways and not develop feelings for him? "You forced me to marry a man I knew nothing about. You make me spy on him and bring you details about his life and business. You all lied to me and told me it was to see if you could trust him, but that wasn't it at all."

"There are things you're better off not knowing."

"What would happen if I backed out and ran away?"

"You wouldn't get very far." He shrugged. "I'm sorry but that's the truth. If you want me to get you out, I will, but you'll have to go into hiding."

"Why?"

"Because if you leave Romero now, he'll know this was a set up, and you won't be safe."

"He won't hurt me."

"You can't live in denial. You've been in his company long enough to know who he is and what he's capable of."

I closed my eyes and thought about that picture Romero showed me of that man. *I know what all of you are capable of.*

"You were in the woods that day when he took out those two men. I bet he didn't even flinch. He killed them without an ounce of remorse, didn't he?"

"None of you are saints."

"Which is exactly why you can't walk away and expect there not to be any consequences. If you want out, I'll help you, but it has to be on my terms. It's the only way I can keep you safe. If we remove you from the situation, our line of communication into your husband's business goes away. How long do you think it will take him to figure out that you were the mole, especially if you up and leave him?"

*I don't want to leave him.*

I couldn't admit that because then my family would think I was turning on them. If I turned on Romero, Rocco would try and protect me, but if I betrayed my family, who would help me? It would only be a matter of time before Romero figured out I was the threat to him.

*I'm fucked.*

"What do you want to do, Lu?" Rocco asked as he took a seat at his desk. "I never wanted you in this situation, but I couldn't go against my father or Vincent."

"I know."

Vincent came into the office and smiled at me, but his presence unsettled me.

"I heard you were here." He stood in front of Rocco's desk. "What's going on?"

"Nothing." I glanced at Rocco, hoping he wouldn't mention my freak out to his brother. "I came for a visit. I have been cooped up in the house, so I thought I'd come and see my family."

"I'm glad you're here," Vincent said. "I was going to call you tonight, but you're getting harder to reach at bedtime."

*That's because my husband keeps me pretty busy.*

"We sent Romero a message a few days ago." Vincent leaned against the desk. "I want to know if he has figured out who sent it."

"Do you want him to know who sent it?" I asked.

"No, but we want to keep him guessing. If we keep him on edge, he'll be vulnerable."

"Why do you want him to be vulnerable?" They were upping their game. "What are you going to do to him?"

"You don't have to worry about that, Luciana," Vincent snapped. "Find out if he knows who sent the message."

"I don't even know what the message was? How am I supposed to know if he talks about it?"

"One of his men went missing a few weeks ago. He was found." Rocco glanced at his brother before continuing. "If Romero talks about the safe house you told us the location of, find out if he knows who would have... find out if he knows we sent the message."

"I gave you the location of the safe house." I pushed the hair from my forehead and gripped it between my fingers. "You sent him a message using his secret location? Of course he'll figure out it was you. And when I say you, I mean *me*."

"I don't think we should send her back," Rocco said. "It's getting too dangerous."

"She has to go back." Vincent raised his voice. "She's married to him. If she doesn't go home, he'll know something's up."

"I said it's too risky." When Rocco stood from his chair, Vincent advanced him.

"Back down," Vincent warned. "We put her in place for a reason. We're not pulling her out now."

"Don't fight." I worked myself between them, facing Rocco. "I have to go back."

"That's our girl." Vincent placed his hand on my shoulder. "You're doing a fantastic job. We're all proud of you."

"I've waited my whole life to hear those words."

Somehow, they weren't as rewarding as I had imagined them to be though. They left me feeling empty and used.

It was a mistake for me to come here because all I did was raise suspicions. As much as Rocco wanted to help me, he couldn't go against his family. If I didn't go back to Romero, he would find me. If I thought I was in the middle of a war now, I'd really be screwed if I ran from both sides.

There was only one way to protect myself. I had to decide who to stand with. It was time to get myself out of this mess once and for all.

∽

THE HOUSE WAS quiet and darker than usual. None of the guys were hurrying in and out of Romero's office, and Gio's car wasn't in the driveway. I had hoped that Romero would be preoccupied with work when I got home. I needed more time to think about how I wanted to approach him.

Should we go on our date? We could have one normal night as husband and wife before I blew up all of this. Should I tell him the truth now? I would beg for his forgiveness and tell him how much I needed him. He would understand the position I was put in by my family. Once he heard it from me, he'd honor his vows and protect me. Wouldn't he?

*Only one way to find out.*

I took my time walking down the hallway to his study. Memories of my uncle coming to get me that morning to tell me what my new role in his family would be cluttered my mind. I remembered feeling alone and afraid when he told me I would be marrying Romero. My cousins said he was cold, ruthless, cruel, and brutal. They warned me I'd have to be careful not to get caught. I had no idea I'd end up falling for him.

Now, I was willingly going to give myself up. What choice did I have? Why did it seem my choices were always so dire? Whatever the outcome was, I was never in the position to come out better on the other side.

If there was anything I had learned over the last few months, it was how to survive. I was so much stronger than I'd thought I was. Whatever the future held for me after tonight, I would find a way out of this. I hoped Romero would stand by my side.

A dull light streamed out of the ajar door of Romero's office. When I stopped in front of it, I willed my shaky hands to settle down. I had to come at my husband from a position of strength. I had to gain his respect and present my case.

*He's going to understand. He has to.*

I'd barely knocked when Romero's deep voice answered.

"Come in, Luciana."

When I pushed open the door, I found Romero sitting in the plush leather chair in the corner of his office. His legs were stretched out in front of him, and he dangled a glass of alcohol over the arm of the chair.

I rubbed my hands over my arms when I entered the frigid room. It seemed like the air conditioner was ten degrees cooler in here than it was in the rest of the house. The chilly air didn't help my trembling body.

He brought his glass to his luscious mouth, taking a long sip of whatever liquid was in there. Maybe I should have him pour me one too. He stared at me over the rim of the glass, his eyes like steel and his facial features hard and tired.

"How was your day?" He finished his drink and set the glass on the floor, never taking his menacing gaze away from mine.

"Better than I thought." I hesitantly came toward him because there was something different in his expression. Maybe it was paranoia, but he looked like he already knew what I wanted to tell him. "How was yours?"

"A little more eventful than I would have liked." When

he got up from the chair, he kicked the glass over. He didn't even look down as it rolled across the floor and stopped when it hit the baseboard under the window. "I received some unsettling news."

"Did you?" I backed away when he came close to me.

"You know how I feel about you retreating from me." He reached for my arm and tugged me toward him. He didn't even flinch when I smacked into his solid chest. "I don't like it."

"I'm sorry." I smoothed my hands along his biceps, breathing in the scent of the alcohol that lingered on his breath. "Do you want to talk about the news you received?"

"Yes, actually I do." He brought me to the chair he had been sitting in and guided me into it. "Do you know how cautious I am with my business? How meticulous I am when it comes to sharing information?"

I grasped the arms of the chair when he trailed his fingers along my neck.

"I choose my soldiers very carefully. They are vetted with top security. I've employed SEALS and ex-police officers. Shit, I even have a former homeland security man among my ranks. You don't get as far as I've gotten without taking all the necessary steps I've taken to secure my position."

"I'm sure you're extremely thorough." I twisted my hands in my lap because I didn't like where this conversation was heading. "What happened?"

"I found out I have a traitor in my house." He gripped my throat in his hand. "What should I do about that?"

## CHAPTER 28

*Romero*

Her breathing sped up when I squeezed her neck in my hand. The tears skimmed her eyes before streaming down her cheeks. Her betrayal hit me like a ton of bricks. No cut of a knife or sting of a bullet piercing through my flesh could injure me worse than the look on her face when she realized I knew the truth.

*Fuck! I wanted Gio to be wrong.*

"Luciana, do you know who the traitor is?"

She sobbed as she nodded.

"I want to hear you say it," I demanded. "If you're brave enough to come into my house and betray me, you should be able to admit it."

"It was me," she cried. "But I didn't want to do it."

"You didn't want to do it?" I shouted as I pushed her against the back of the chair, squeezing her throat tighter than I should have. "What the fuck does that mean?"

"Please," she said, clawing against my hand, but I didn't release her. "Stop."

I got on top of her, placing my knees on either side of

her waist. It would be so easy for me to snuff the life out of her. She would deserve it for what she had done to me.

Her terrified gaze only strengthened my will to continue. How had she pulled this off? How had I let her? I'd bought her innocent act. I'd believed her family put her in my path because they cared so little about her, but that wasn't it at all. She was just like the rest of them. She came here to set me up, and that would have dire consequences.

She pulled at my wrist, trying to get me to let go of her.

When I released her from my violent hold, my fingers left behind red marks. That would be a reminder to us both of what I truly was. What I was capable of doing to her. She gasped for air, but she didn't try to push me away. Her chest heaved up and down and her body shook in terror.

"Give me one fucking reason why I shouldn't snap your neck and send you back to your uncle in a body bag?"

"Because," she whispered as the tears poured out of her eyes, "I love you."

"You love me?" I laughed at the absurdity of that statement. "What the hell am I supposed to do with that?"

"Maybe not laugh at me and let me explain."

"The floor is all yours, butterfly."

After I got off her, I took my gun out of the back of my waistband and placed it on my desk in her sight, so she didn't forget what I could do if I didn't like her explanation.

She shifted in her seat, fidgeting with her hands as she glanced at my gun.

"You're running out of time," I said. "I'm all out of patience when it comes to you."

"I didn't want to do any of this," she said. "I didn't want to marry you, but they told me I had to. They told me this was an assignment, but I had no idea how far in I would become. I didn't expect to like you, let alone fall for you."

"So, you're telling me they made you do this. They didn't give you a choice?"

"Not at all." She wiped her face, smearing her mascara underneath her eyes. "They told me they needed to know if they could trust you before working with you. I was supposed to spy on you and make sure you weren't betraying them."

"That doesn't make any sense. There would be no reason for me to betray them. They approached me."

"I didn't know any of that. I trusted what they said, but I realized soon after that they wanted me to bring them information about you and your business. They weren't trying to gauge your trust. They were trying to bring you down."

That would never happen. They weren't going to live long enough to take anything from me. I would make them pay. All of them.

"I thought about running, but where would I go? They would find me, and once I became your wife, I couldn't leave. You would have come after me too. I was stuck in a horrible situation. I couldn't say no to my family, but I couldn't pretend to be your wife either."

"What do you mean?"

"Our wedding night was real for me."

I didn't want to believe her. I wouldn't allow her to suck me into her lies.

"Why do you think I was so mad at you the next day? You left me alone and vulnerable. I had no idea how to process what we had done. I needed you to stay with me that night. And then, you took me to that business meeting and made me watch as you killed two people. I was terrified of you, but I had to stay and do what my family asked of me."

"You could have come to me. I would have protected you."

"The same way my family protects me? I hate them for thinking they could put me in this situation and expect me to be with you as your wife and not develop feelings for you. They made me betray you and I let them."

"You didn't give me a chance, Luciana." I moved toward the chair and to my surprise, she didn't cower when I dropped to my knees in front of her. "I told you on our wedding day, I wanted to try to make this real, but you had no intentions of ever doing that."

"I was too afraid."

When she stroked my face, it was me who retreated, grabbing her wrist and backing away from her touch. I had to stay in control if I was going to get through any of this.

"You fucking hurt me." Why did I admit that?

"I know."

"I don't forgive." I tightened my hold on her wrist. "Anyone who has ever betrayed me hasn't lived to tell."

"I was going to tell you today."

"That's convenient considering I exposed you today." I rested my free hand on her thigh. "When I found out what you had done, my first instinct was to kill you."

I slithered my hand under her skirt and toyed with the elastic of her panties. "Then I thought, that would be too quick. Too good for you."

She spread her legs when I slipped my fingers inside her panties and ran them along her slit.

"I don't know if I should be flattered or offended that you're this aroused," I said. "I thought you'd be too afraid of me to let me touch you."

"I don't want to be afraid of you."

"You might have to live with both the arousal and the

fear." I fingered her as I brought my lips to her neck and kissed her heated flesh. "Killing you would be too easy."

"Romero," she moaned.

"What I have in mind is going to be far more advantageous." I withdrew my fingers from her wet pussy. "For me, at least."

"What do you want?"

"Everything." When I ripped open her blouse, the buttons flew in the air and bounced off the floor. "Starting with you."

I reached under her skirt and tugged her panties down her legs, and then tossed them over my shoulder.

"You said you won't forgive me."

I pressed my lips against her flat stomach and kissed my way to her breasts, reaching behind her and unclasping her bra. Taking her breasts in my hands, I squeezed them as I licked and bit her nipples.

"I'm not going to forgive you." I continued to feast on her glorious tits, torturing her nipples with my tongue and teeth. "You don't deserve my forgiveness."

"Then stop this." She pushed at my shoulder. "Let me go."

"No." I pushed her skirt up, exposing her bare sex to me. "I'll never let you go."

"I don't understand. You still want to be married to me?"

"Being married to you is the best position I can be in." I glanced between her thighs and licked my lips. "I can ride you to the edge of pleasure every night."

I lowered my head between her legs and kissed her silky inner thigh.

She gripped my hair in her hands and guided me closer to her. I granted her wish, and flattened my tongue along her entrance, tasting her sweet arousal.

"Romero." She bucked her hips forward. "Please forgive me."

I lifted my head up and gazed at her from between her legs. "I can't do that, baby, but I have come up with a solution on how you're going to make all of this up to me."

"How?"

I kissed my way up her stomach, then swirled my tongue around her nipples as I pushed my fingers inside her.

She squeezed her legs shut and rode my hand with a quick thrust of her hips.

"You're going to do for me exactly what you did for your family."

"What?" When her eyes flew open, they were filled with terror. That aroused me. "No, I don't want to do that."

"If you thought saying no to your family was a mistake, then you have no idea what I'm capable of." I kissed her hard on the mouth as I drove my fingers deep inside her. "I said I wouldn't kill you, but I didn't say anything about your family."

She shook her head, but she couldn't stop rocking against my hand. My touch was far too addicting to her, and that would be my advantage.

"I know you don't care about your aunt and uncle, and probably not even Vincent." I nodded toward my gun. "But I do know you wouldn't want me to put a bullet between Sandro or Rocco's eyes."

"No, please."

"It's all up to you, Luciana." I withdrew my fingers and licked them before running them along her full lips. "It will be like a twisted game of Russian Roulette. You won't know which one of them the bullet is for until it's done."

"You're sick."

"If I'm so sick, why are you dripping for me?"

She closed her eyes, hiding her shame.

"Look at me." I gripped her chin in my hand. "You belong to me in every sense of the word. You can't go back to your family because once they find out I know what you were here to do, they'll dispose of you and come after me."

I traced my finger over her nipple. "If they come for me, I'll kill them all. No mercy."

"I didn't want to do this to you."

"You did it anyway." I move my finger down her stomach, running it around her belly button, and then over her mound. "I know how much you want this."

I pushed my fingers inside her.

"None of that has to change." I added a third finger, making her scream out for more. "All you have to do is get me information on your family and feed them what I tell you to."

"God." She dropped her head on the back of the chair and shoved her pelvis forward. "Please."

"I'm a fair man." I continued to finger her. "If you do what I say and get me what I want, I'll make sure you get what you want."

With one hand buried between her legs, I twisted my fingers through her hair and tugged her face to mine. Biting her lip, I drew blood, delighting in the taste of the coppery liquid on my tongue. She cried out, but not from pain. She quivered and thrashed against my hand, releasing her hot, forbidden fluid all over my fingers.

While she tried to catch her breath, I kissed her hard, making sure she understood her new mission.

"Say you belong to me," I demanded, my fingers still buried inside her.

"I ..." She swallowed back her fear. "I belong to you."

"That's my girl." I kissed her softer this time. "You'll do what I say."

"Yes."

"You're going to help me bring down the Torrios. It's the only way you can make up for your deception."

I didn't think she could ever make up for it, but this was a start. She had no idea how difficult it was for me to push back my pride and let her live. As much as I hated to admit it, I had fallen for her too. And now, in the chaos and brutality of our lives, our twisted love story was only beginning.

"Now you are my prisoner, my little butterfly."

The End.

Continue on with this dark, edgy series to see if Luciana can really do what Romero expects of her in *Her Heartless King*.

My Book

## HER HEARTLESS KING

*No one can survive torn between two ruthless mafia families. But that's exactly where I find myself.*

I made a grave mistake when I agreed to spy on my new husband for my family.

I thought it was a way to take my place in this brutal life I never asked for.

But then the unthinkable happened...

I fell in love with him, and I never imagined my betrayal would have so many consequences.

Now, I'm his prisoner, and he expects me to turn the tables on my family and betray them the way I did him.

Each bit of information I bring him grants me access to his touch, his kiss, and his body I so shamelessly crave.

Romero awakens my desires, and the lust that sparks between us can only be quenched when he gives me what I need.

The lies and the secrets are tearing me apart, and I have to decide between the loyalty I owe my family or the man who has awakened my fire for life.

Either choice is a death sentence.
Continue on with the riveting second part of *The Sold To The Mafia Boss Series*.
My Book

## ABOUT THE AUTHOR

USA Today Bestselling author Ella Jade writes dark mafia romances with dominating mob bosses, the strong women who challenge them, and suspenseful twists that keep her readers turning the pages.

When she isn't reading or writing sexy, angsty, and intense words, she indulges in a well-crafted martini and binge watches episodes of Dallas, Falcon Crest, and Dynasty, where she learned at an early age how to spin an old-school cliffhanger. She also enjoys spoiling her two chihuahua writing companions.

For all the news about upcoming releases and what she's creating next, subscribe to Ella's newsletter.

Sign up for her newsletter here:
https://view.flodesk.com/pages/5eaf17b582272f0026fed03a

Printed in Great Britain
by Amazon